DOUBLE IDENTITY
DIANE BURKE

Steeple
Hill®

Published by Steeple Hill Books™

STEEPLE HILL BOOKS

Steeple
Hill®

Recycling programs
for this product may
not exist in your area.

ISBN-13: 978-0-373-44435-9

DOUBLE IDENTITY

www.SteepleHill.com

Printed in U.S.A.

Be humble and gentle.
Be patient with each other, making allowances
for each other's faults because of your love.
— *Ephesians* 4:2

To Michele,
a wonderful and warm new addition to our family.
You had just the right touch of enthusiasm,
encouragement and gentle prodding
to keep me at the keyboard.

And

a special thanks to Vincent Gimmelli,
nephew of my heart, who let me borrow his name.

ONE

"According to this report, Miss Clarkston, you do not exist."

Cain Garrison looked up from the file folder lying on his desk. He had to admit he was intrigued. It had been quite a while since anyone had contracted his private investigator services for anything more than getting the goods on a cheating husband or following up on insurance fraud. Usually, it was so quiet in the small town of Promise, Virginia, that he found most of his work in neighboring counties or in the city of Charlottesville.

Tapping his index finger on the folder, he said, "Your birth certificate and social security card are phony." His eyes locked with hers. "Okay, I'll take the bait. Who are you really and what do you want from me?"

He leaned back in his chair and studied the petite young woman sitting in front of him. If he had to guess, he'd say she was in her early twenties. Thick ebony hair covered her shoulders and trailed down her back. She wore a T-shirt, jeans, sneakers and little, if any, makeup. But then she didn't need any.

She squared her shoulders. He might have bought into her calm-and-collected facade if he hadn't noticed her ramrod straight posture as she perched on the edge of her chair and her white knuckles from the tight clasp of her hands.

"My name is Sophia Joy Clarkston but everybody calls me Sophie. I was born twenty-two years ago to Elizabeth and Anthony Clarkston. My mother died in a car accident shortly after I was born. My dad raised me." Her lips pursed in distaste and she nodded toward the folder on his desk. "I don't care what lies are written on that piece of paper. I know who I am. I need you to find my dad."

Ahh, the plot thickens. Cain tried to hide the smile pulling at his lips. This must be his sister's idea of a prank. He'd been complaining lately about being bored. Voilà. Phony case that she knew he'd salivate over. Okay, he'd play the game. Why not?

"Your dad's missing?"

Sophie chewed on her bottom lip and nodded. She smoothed her jeans, picking at pretend lint, trying unsuccessfully to hide her nervousness.

"Adults aren't usually considered missing, Miss Clarkston. My experience has taught me most people leave of their own volition, mostly because they're just tired of being where they are or with the people around them. How long ago did your father disappear and what makes you think this qualifies as a missing person case?"

"He's been gone two weeks now." She rummaged in the tote bag resting at her feet and withdrew a white piece of paper. "I received this letter a couple of days after he left."

Cain reached across the desk and accepted the letter from her hand. He knew from the crinkled and stained condition of the paper that the note had probably been crushed into a ball, tossed in the trash, only to be rescued, folded and put away for safekeeping. If the variety of stains meant anything, he was pretty sure this note had hit the trash can more than once. Whatever the contents, one thing was evident. This letter had created a seesaw of emotions in this woman.

He read the first line. He blinked hard and then read the first line again.

By the time you get this letter, I'll be dead.

Cain shot a look to Sophie. Sea-foam green eyes shimmering with an ocean depth of emotions stared back at him. Maybe this wasn't a prank. He focused his attention on the paper in his hands.

Sophie studied the man's face as he read the letter—again—for the third, maybe fourth time. His chiseled features revealed none of his thoughts or emotions. For all intents and purposes, it was easy to pretend he was one of her sculptures. An inanimate object, consisting of carved angles and sharp edges, incapable of emotion.

Unless, like herself, he'd learned how to bury those emotions.

She'd read the letter at least a hundred times in the past two weeks. It still had the power to make her feel like someone was physically ripping her heart out of her chest. What had her dad been thinking? Why hadn't he confided in her? Trusted her? Maybe she could have helped him.

A flush of anger swept over her. Didn't he know how frightened and worried she'd be at his sudden disappearance? How could he have done this to her? Just as quickly she was filled with remorse. She shouldn't be mad at him. Obviously, he wasn't thinking clearly. He was in trouble. Desperate and feeling alone. Pretty much like she was feeling right about now.

Sophie steadied her trembling hands. She needed to stay levelheaded. She refused to believe her dad was dead. If he was, she'd know, wouldn't she? There'd be a huge, aching void where her heart had been. Instead, all she felt was pain, fear and confusion.

He had to be alive. Nothing else was acceptable or comprehendible. She had to find him before his words came true.

She drew in a deep, calming breath and tried to remain patient while the investigator continued reading. His body language indicated he was intrigued by the document in his hand. Subtle movements. Chewing his lower lip as he read. Fingers drumming a steady rhythm against the arm of his chair. A slight squinting of his eyes, fanning lines across his skin. How many times was he going to read the letter? She could recite it for him if he wanted. She knew each word by heart.

I am enclosing this gift as a token of my love.

Sophie's hand flew to the hand-carved wooden heart hanging around her neck. Her fingers traced an idle path along the intricate design.

I know you don't understand why I left without a word. But for your safety, I could not tell you then and don't dare tell you now.

For my safety? Mine?

Oh, Dad. What's going on? What do you mean you'll be dead? You can't be dead. You can't.

They're coming. I must hurry and say good-bye.

I am ready, princess. I am ready to go on that last great adventure each one of us inevitably takes.

Just know that I love you...with all my heart.

Her breathing quickened and her eyes flew to Cain Garrison. Was he going to take the case? She didn't know what she'd do if he turned her down. Would he be able to help? She'd tried everything she could think of and he was her last hope. She fidgeted in her seat. How much longer would he sit there staring at that rotten piece of paper that had caused her nothing but sorrow and anger?

Dear Lord, help me be patient. After all, I've had time to digest this nightmare. This man's had about six minutes.

The prayer came automatically, almost as if her mind didn't remember that she had stopped talking to God. He didn't answer prayers…or, at least, He didn't answer hers.

Sophie brushed her hair off her shoulders, letting it fall in waves down her back, and sat straighter in the soft leather chair. She could almost hear her dad's scolding voice from childhood. "Sophie Joy Clarkston, what's wrong with you? You're full of itches and twitches, girl."

Itches and twitches.

Sophie chewed on a fingernail and thought about the last time she'd seen her dad. After a late dinner they'd sat together on the front porch, listening to music, gazing at the stars, sharing idle conversation. She'd kissed him good-night and gone up to bed. The next morning she'd found a bag filled with money—a huge sum of money—lying on the table by her chair. He was gone. Without warning or word of any kind. Until two days later when the letter had arrived in the mail.

Her breath came in short, quick gasps and she felt like she was going to crawl out of her skin. She needed to distract herself. Fast.

Crossing to the window, she raised a slat and looked outside. Main Street consisted of four blocks of mom-and-pop stores, a restaurant or two, an insurance company, a pharmacy. A handful of passersby bustled past the window as they hurried about their business. A few people stood together on the sidewalk chatting.

Nothing scary.

Nothing ominous.

So why couldn't she shake the feeling that someone was watching her every move? Her nerves were shot. She hadn't had a good night's sleep in weeks and it was starting to show.

"Forgive my rudeness, Ms. Clarkston," Cain said as he

placed the letter on his desk and stood. "Can I offer you a cup of coffee or a soft drink?"

"Coffee would be wonderful. Cream and sugar, please. And call me Sophie."

Blinking hard to hold back tears, she returned to her chair. She admired the professional yet welcoming atmosphere of the office as she looked around. Two brown leather chairs faced a highly polished mahogany desk. The tall cabinet on the far wall looked more like a fine piece of furniture than storage for files. A variety of plants and a large silk tree added an outdoor ambience to the room. Two framed professional investigator licenses hung on the wall to the left of heavy hunter-green drapes.

Two? In such a small town as Promise?

The deep, rich aroma of freshly ground coffee wafted from behind a silk screen standing in front of a small kitchen area. Sophie's stomach growled, reminding her she hadn't had any breakfast…or dinner the night before.

"One sugar or two?"

Sophie liked listening to the deep resonant tone of his voice. He seemed sure of himself, in control. And that's what she needed right now, someone to help control the chaos surrounding her.

"Two, please."

She watched him approach. His thick chestnut hair tumbled in an unkempt wave across his forehead, almost obscuring his vision, and she had to sit on her hands to control the absurd impulse she had to reach up and swipe it out of his eyes. He was handsome, sort of a young Johnny Depp look-alike, late twenties, maybe early thirties. If he was as good at his job as he was to look at, then she was definitely in the right place.

Cain winced as he carried the coffee mug to his client. The stiffness in his left leg shot a wave of pain into his hip.

He could feel her eyes boring into him as he limped across the room.

"Don't worry. It looks a lot worse than it is." He grinned and handed her a mug.

"I'm sorry. I didn't mean to stare."

"Don't sweat it. You're simply wondering if you're spending your money wisely or if you've made a mistake."

"It's not that," she stammered.

"Of course it is." He grinned and perched his hip on the edge of the desk. "Never apologize for considering all the facts when making a business transaction." He slapped his leg. "I could joke and say it's an old war injury. In a way it probably is. A war wound from my undercover narcotics days when I worked for the Charlottesville police."

"I'm sorry."

"Don't be. You didn't do it." He slid off the edge of the desk and went back to his chair. "After my injury, they offered me a life behind a desk but that wasn't the life for me." He rapped on the desk. "Unless I own the desk, of course."

Her smile made him happy that his words had had their desired effect.

"How long have you been a private investigator?" Sophie asked.

"Three years now. My partner and I opened Garrison Investigations shortly after I moved back home. I decided I'd had enough of big-city living and wanted to return to my country roots."

"Pardon my rudeness, but I'm surprised you have a partner, Mr. Garrison. If I remember correctly, Promise is a very small town."

Cain grinned. "That's so true, Ms. Clarkston."

"Sophie…"

He nodded. "Sophie. My sister, Holly, is my partner. She runs the diner across the street. Serves the best home-cooked meals you've ever tasted. But every now and then when I run into a situation where a female touch would have more success, she steps in and helps out."

Sophie nodded her understanding.

He leaned back in his chair. "How did you hear about us? Yellow pages? Word of mouth?"

"You're listed in the Crossroads Church business directory."

"You attend Crossroads? I don't remember seeing you there. Not that I know everyone, of course, but it is a small community and newcomers have a tendency to be noticed."

"I haven't attended really. I've just arrived in town." She shifted in her seat, her eyes downcast. "Besides, the Lord and I aren't on speaking terms these days."

Cain tented his fingers in front of his lips to hide his smile. "That so? Yet you chose to get your business references from the church directory instead of the yellow pages?"

Color heightened in her cheeks.

"Where are you from?" Cain asked.

A shadow of hesitation crossed her face. "I'm a bit of a nomad. I don't call any one place home."

Cain tilted his head to the side and studied her bowed head. There were many layers and hidden secrets to Miss Sophie Clarkston. She intrigued him.

"Well, let me be one of the first to welcome you to Promise. I'm surprised you found us," he said. "But I'm glad you did."

"I'm familiar with Promise, Mr. Garrison. My family has owned a small cottage about ten miles out of town for as long as I can remember. My dad and I travel extensively so we rarely stay in it, but if I had to call one place home, I guess Promise would qualify."

Cain rested his forearms on his desk. "Tell me about this letter."

She sipped her coffee then placed the mug on the desk. "I received the letter two days after my dad disappeared. The postmark made me think he came to the cottage. If he did, he didn't stay."

The pain he saw in her eyes stirred him.

"Has your father ever done anything like this before?"

"No. Definitely not. My father would never hurt me."

Cain didn't bother to point out that that is exactly what he had just done.

"It's always been just me and my dad," Sophie said. "He's hardworking, kind, loving. He has a strong belief in God and lives his life modeling his faith. I don't understand. He never would have left me without a word. Never. Unless he had no other choice. I need your help, Mr. Garrison. I need to know what happened to my dad."

"Call me Cain. In this small town, Mr. Garrison is still my father's name." He grabbed a tablet and pen out of his side desk drawer. "Why don't we start at the beginning?" He made a few notations on the paper and asked without looking up, "I assume when your dad disappeared you notified the police." Her hesitation caused him to look up.

"Yes." She squirmed in her seat and didn't make eye contact with him. "At first, they weren't much help. It's not against the law for an adult to decide to leave. When I got this letter, I tried to convince them that he was in danger and we needed to find him."

"And?"

"They still didn't seem to take it very seriously. They wrote up a missing person's report. One of the officers was really nice. He promised me he'd look into it and he did." Her eyes cut to his. "That's how I found out my identification papers are phony. So are my dad's. They weren't able to find anything after that. Truthfully, I think they just stopped trying."

He lowered his pen and sat back. Something wasn't right

here. She was holding something back. He sensed it and wondered why.

"Sophie…" Cain ran his hand through his thick brown hair and tried to choose his words so as not to cause her any more pain. "I understand this whole situation has been very difficult for you."

"Difficult? It's been a living nightmare. Every memory I ever had, every single thing I thought I knew about myself and my dad is now nothing more than questions. I need to know what's going on."

"You're going to need more help than I can give. I'm a small-town investigator. My biggest cases are insurance fraud, cheating spouses and missing pets. You should contract a larger investigation firm in the city. They'd have more resources than me."

Sophie fought back tears. "What big city would you recommend, Cain? I can't remember ever setting foot in a city, any city, until two weeks ago. And since we've moved from one small town to another for the past twenty-two years, what city or town do you suggest I call home?" She tapped her index finger on the file folder lying on his desk. "Besides, this report was done by big-city cops. Your old stomping ground, as a matter of fact. The Charlottesville police discovered the documents I had were fake."

The quiet desperation underlying her words filled him with empathy. Cain offered a silent prayer for wisdom on how he could help this woman.

"Do you have anything else that might indicate your father's true identity? Maybe an entry in a family Bible or a name on the back of a photograph? Anything at all to give me a place to start?"

She shook her head.

Thoughts ricocheted like pinballs through his mind. "What about the cottage?" He leaned forward and rested his forearms on the desk. "You said it had been in your family for years. There must be legal documents to prove it. A real estate title, for one."

Sophie shrugged. "Maybe. Like I told you, we've owned it for as long as I can remember. I have no idea if there are any papers to prove it. I just figured possession is nine tenths of the law." She held up an object in her hand. "I have the key."

A smile danced across her lips and Cain's heart skipped a beat. There was something about her, a vulnerability hidden beneath resilience, a shyness buried beneath determination, that drew him to her.

He'd promised himself never again—never get emotionally involved with a woman on one of his cases. He'd learned his lesson the hard way and vowed never to repeat it. This unexpected empathy he felt was unsettling.

She needed his help. And he needed a new client. So he'd help her, despite the fact that fake documents would make it an uphill battle all the way. He'd just have to make sure this time that he used his head, kept things strictly professional between them. He couldn't afford to allow himself to have any feelings for her…not even empathy. He had no intention of walking down that treacherous path a second time.

Cain crossed around the desk, plopped in the leather chair beside her and clasped his hands between his knees. "I know how hard this must be on you," he said, leaning forward and locking his gaze with hers. "And I'll do what I can to help. But I've got to be honest here. You're probably throwing your money away. Fake identities usually lead to dead ends."

She stood and offered him her hand. "I understand. Thank you for your honesty."

He clasped her hand in his. He couldn't bear the look of defeat in her eyes. "I'll tell you what I'll do." He stood. "Leave me your address. I'll see if I can locate a real estate title on the property. And I'll include it in the consultation fee you just paid so it won't cost you any more money. Meanwhile, I want you to go home and look through anything and everything you own for a name, an address, a picture. Anything you think might give me a place to start looking. You find something and we'll talk again."

"Thanks." She scribbled her address on a scrap of paper she pulled from her tote bag and handed it to him.

"Wait a minute," he called as she crossed the room.

Sophie turned and paused in the doorway.

"At least let me take you to Holly's for a welcome-to-Promise lunch."

Yeah, that's professional. That's keeping your distance. Invite the client to lunch because she looks at you with lost puppy dog eyes. Are you crazy?

"Taking a client to lunch counts as a business deduction on my taxes. So, believe it or not, you'll actually be helping me out." The words tumbled from his mouth even though his brain kept screaming, *Idiot! Let somebody else feel sorry for her.*

"Just let me know what day is good for you," he continued. "My sister makes the best apple pie you've ever tasted."

Sophie smiled and when she did it lit up the room. "Sure. I'll see you around."

Cain crossed to the window and watched as Sophie exited the building. She stopped to help elderly Mrs. Gleason, whose grocery bag had split open. Sophie was chasing oranges along the sidewalk when a movement out of the corner of Cain's eye caught his attention. A man stood in the shadows of the alley a block up the street. From this distance, Cain could only see the man's silhouette and the tip of a lit cigarette but something about his stealth caught and held his attention. As soon as the man spotted Sophie, he threw his cigarette to the ground and hopped into a car parked beside him.

Cain glanced back to Sophie. Her hair blew across her mouth and she laughingly wiped it away as she handed the last of the runaway oranges to Mrs. Gleason. With a smile and a wave, Sophie turned to step into the street.

The car barreled out of the alley.

"Sophie!" Cain banged on the glass to get her attention but she was already stepping into the street.

The car accelerated.

Lord, help me, please.

Cain raced for the door.

TWO

A freight train slammed into Sophie's back. At least it felt like it, as an unexpected force knocked her off her feet and propelled her forward into midair. As she stretched out her hands to break her fall, she felt two arms wrap around her middle, spin her around, and then someone slid beneath her, cushioning her slide across the asphalt.

When the momentum stopped, Sophie found herself staring up at the clouds and wondering what had just happened. Before she could move a muscle, the ground beneath her shifted, someone clasped her waist, lifted her and then gently lowered her so that she was lying on the street.

"Sophie, don't move. Are you hurt? Is anything broken?"

She shielded her eyes against the sun with her hand and tried to identify the hulking form leaning over her.

"Cain?" She shifted her weight and a groan escaped her lips when she tried to sit up.

A crowd began gathering around them.

"Cain, are you okay?" A man, older but strikingly similar in appearance to Cain, placed a hand on Cain's shoulder. "I called it in. Help should be here in a minute."

"Thanks, Dad."

Mrs. Gleason, the woman Sophie had helped with her

groceries, stood beside them wringing her hands and saying, "I can't believe it. I saw the whole thing. That car missed you by inches. You could have been killed."

"Car?" Sophie tried again to sit up.

"No. Don't move until the ambulance gets here," Cain said.

"Ambulance?" She glanced at the faces looming over her and then pushed Cain's hand away and sat up. "No. Please. I don't need an ambulance."

When he saw she was determined to stand, he helped her to her feet.

"What happened?" she asked.

"A black car tried to run you down, that's what happened." The elderly woman raised her voice so the bystanders could hear. "This young man ran out of that building and pushed you out of the way. I saw the whole thing."

A smile tugged at the corner of Sophie's mouth as the older woman recounted the incident—and Sophie was sure Mrs. Gleason would tell it again and again before the day was through.

Sophie's legs trembled, rebelling at the idea of supporting her weight, and she leaned heavily against Cain as they made their way through the crowd to the curb.

"A car tried to run me down?" she asked, looking up at Cain. "What car?"

"It was a big, black car." Mrs. Gleason patted Sophie's arm as she accompanied them to the sidewalk. "The driver came shooting out of the alley by the pharmacy. He must have lost control or something because he headed right for you." She picked up her grocery bags from the sidewalk. "The whole thing scared five years off this old ticker of mine."

Sophie's head pounded and her right forearm burned from road rash. Otherwise, she hadn't sustained any injuries. With effort, she smiled at the older woman. "I'm so sorry I scared you. But I'm fine. Really."

The air hummed with spectator whispers. An ambulance and a police car, approaching from opposite directions, slid up to the curb.

Cain's breath fanned the back of Sophie's neck and his arm cradled her shoulders, lending his support as they stood together on the sidewalk. The sheriff reached them first.

Sheriff Dalton nodded at Cain and doffed his hat at Sophie. "Ma'am, can you tell me what happened here?"

"I can tell you, Sheriff. I saw the whole thing." Mrs. Gleason waved her hand excitedly.

"I appreciate that, Mrs. Gleason," the sheriff replied, gently steering the woman and her bag of groceries down the street. "Why don't you go over to the office and be the first one to tell Sally all about it. I'll be over shortly and take your formal statement."

Mrs. Gleason didn't have to be asked twice. Shoulders tossed back and strutting with an air of self-importance, she hurried down the street.

The paramedics approached and made a cursory exam of both Cain and Sophie.

"We're fine," Cain said. "A few bumps and skin tears but nothing some peroxide and a bandage or two won't cure."

"Okay," said Mr. Garrison. "Let's get you both inside and I'll have the two of you fixed up in no time."

Thanking the paramedics before dismissing them, Cain and Sophie followed Mr. Garrison inside Cain's office. Sheriff Dalton trailed close behind. Sophie allowed herself to wallow in the warmth of Cain's body as he ushered her inside the building. She couldn't be sure if it was the adrenaline rush from the near hit-and-run or the unexpected nearness of Cain Garrison that caused her stomach to flip-flop and her pulse to race.

Within seconds she was seated in the same leather chair she had left only minutes before.

Cain handed her a bottle of water.

She took a long gulp and welcomed the cold liquid as it slid down her dry throat.

Cain pulled a chair over to face her and leaned his forearms on his thighs. His worried expression creased deep lines near his mouth and at the corners of his eyes.

Mr. Garrison opened a first aid kit and took out a bottle of hydrogen peroxide, tape, gauze and a few smaller bandages.

Sheriff Dalton flipped his notepad open. "So which one of you is gonna tell me what happened?"

"I don't know what happened," Sophie answered honestly. "One minute I was crossing the street and the next I was flying through the air."

Cain laughed out loud. "Yeah, I can see how you'd think that." He turned his attention to the sheriff. "I was looking out my office window when I saw a black sedan shoot out of the alley and head right for Sophie…er, Miss Clarkston. I banged on the window to warn her but when I realized she hadn't heard, I ran outside and pushed her out of the way."

Sheriff Dalton eyed Sophie. "Do you know any reason why someone would be trying to run you down?"

Sophie shook her head.

"What kind of car was it?" the sheriff asked.

"Black sedan. Unfortunately, I didn't get a good enough look to be able to tell you anything else," Cain said.

"And you just happened to be looking out your window when you saw all this going down?" The sheriff pushed his hat back on his head, his expression skeptical.

"Miss Clarkston had just left my office."

Sheriff Dalton looked at Sophie, shot a glance at Cain and

grinned as though all of a sudden the reason Cain had been staring out the window at Sophie was pretty evident.

"Is Miss Clarkston a client?"

"Yes."

The sheriff pursed his lips. "Whatever investigating you're having done, Ms. Clarkston, do you think it could make someone mad enough to try and run you over with their car?"

Sophie shrugged. "I can't imagine anyone wanting to hurt me, Sheriff, for any reason."

Mr. Garrison dressed Sophie's arm and then turned his attention to his son's skin tears.

Sheriff Dalton slipped his notepad back into his shirt pocket. "Well, there's not much to go on. But I'll ask around. Maybe somebody saw the make and model or got some of the license plate numbers." He crossed the room. "If either of you think of anything that might be helpful, you know where to get in touch with me."

As the sheriff slipped out the door, he was almost knocked over by a person trying to shove him aside.

"Cain!" The woman burst into the room. "I just heard. Are you okay? I can't believe you jumped in front of a car. Are you crazy?"

She ran her hands over Cain's shoulders and down his arms, obviously checking for injuries. Her fingers cradled his chin and she grimaced at the scrape across his cheek. Her touch seemed possessive, familiar.

His wife? Girlfriend?

The tiniest twinge of jealousy stabbed at Sophie and her eyes widened in surprise.

Jealous? Over a man she'd just met? Couldn't be.

No, the twinges of envy nagging at her were because he had someone to care about him and she didn't.

She loved her father, but their nomadic lifestyle had robbed her of the opportunity to make any long, lasting friendships or date anyone more than once or twice. It had been a very lonely existence. And now that her father had vanished she found herself facing what she feared the most—being totally alone in the world.

"Were you hurt?" The woman tilted Cain's face up. "You're going to have a shiner, all right. You idiot. You could have been killed."

"That's enough, Holly," Mr. Garrison said. "Cain's been through enough today."

Sophie quietly studied the woman. She wore blue jeans and a pink T-shirt. Her hair circled her face in tight brown curls. She was a pretty girl and appeared to be about Sophie's age.

Cain removed the woman's hands from his face and stood up. He towered about six inches over her. "I'm fine, Holly. Calm down. How did you find out so fast, anyway?"

"Mrs. Gleason told Mrs. Summit who told Mac who came in the diner and told me."

Cain shook his head from side to side. "Small towns," he muttered under his breath.

Sophie shifted in her seat. The movement caught the woman's attention. "Who's this?" she asked, directing her question to Cain but not taking her eyes off Sophie.

"Hi. I'm Sophie. I'd offer to shake your hand but mine is covered with antibiotic cream." Sophie held her hand up.

"This is our newest client," Cain said. He turned his head and grinned at Sophie. "This is my sister, Holly." He inclined his head toward the licenses hanging on the office wall. "And my partner."

Sister? Partner? Sophie grinned. *Not wife or girlfriend? Isn't that interesting.* And she found herself wondering why the knowledge that Cain was single made her feel all warm and fuzzy.

"Your brother saved my life," Sophie said. "I'm shuddering

just thinking about how much he plans to bill me for services above and beyond the norm."

Holly grinned and hopped up on the edge of the desk. "Nice to meet you. Sorry for the way I burst in the door. It's just…"

"Don't sweat it. I understand. I'd be upset, too, if my brother jumped in front of a moving car. If I had a brother, that is."

"So, who's the dude with the lead foot?" Holly asked. "Ex-boyfriend? Ex-husband? Current husband?"

"Holly, knock it off," Cain chided.

"What? She must have hired you for something that made somebody mad. It's a logical conclusion."

Mr. Garrison laughed out loud. "Holly and the word *logic* in the same sentence? Wait until I tell your mother." He closed the first aid kit and headed for the door. "Will you be coming over for dinner, son? You know as soon as your mother gets wind of this she's going to be all over me for answers."

Cain shook his head. "Sorry, Dad. Holly can fill her in. I'm going to run Sophie home."

"That's not necessary," Sophie interjected. "My car is parked across the street."

"Don't worry about your car. My sister can drive it out first thing in the morning. I'll follow her and we'll ride back to town together."

"But I can drive…"

"Sure you can," Cain said. "But it is southern hospitality to make sure a young lady gets home in one piece…particularly after she hired you to work for her and then almost got run down right in front of your place of business. Besides, do you really want to grip a steering wheel with scraped hands?"

Sophie paused for a moment and looked at the three people staring at her. For the first time in weeks, she didn't feel alone.

They were going to help her. Suddenly the heavy weight she'd been carrying felt lighter.

"Thanks, Cain. Holly. Mr. Garrison." A warm glow washed over her from head to toe.

Mr. Garrison nodded and slipped out the door.

Sophie was too stubborn to offer up the silent prayer of gratitude that rested on the tip of her tongue. She was still mad at God. Sometimes she thought she always would be. But a little voice inside her head told her He already knew her heart.

"So, you're our new client." Holly gave her the once-over. "Please tell me you didn't hire us to follow a cheating husband. Someone as pretty and sweet as you shouldn't be married to a no-account."

Sophie laughed. "I'm not married." The smile fell from her lips. "I hired your firm to investigate my missing father."

"Your father? Wow, that stinks. When did he disappear?"

"Two weeks ago."

"And the police?"

"They didn't find anything useful." Sophie sighed. "I'm sorry, Holly. I really don't feel up to going over all of it again." She pressed her fingers to her forehead and rubbed little circles against her skin in an attempt to stop the pounding. "Cain has all the information. Would you mind terribly if I let him fill you in?"

"Sure. What am I thinking? I'm the one who needs to apologize. You almost got run over. I'd say that's more than enough to deal with for one day." Holly rummaged in the first aid kit and then held out two pills and a glass of water. "Here. This should help with that headache."

"Thanks."

"Don't worry," Cain assured her. "All you need is a good

night's sleep." He cupped her elbow and helped Sophie to her feet. "C'mon, let's get you home."

As Sophie stood, her stomach growled loudly enough to draw attention. Her cheeks flamed with embarrassment and Holly and Cain laughed.

"Sounds like you could use a good, hot meal." Holly spoke to Cain as she headed for the door. "I've gotta run. I left Phil in charge of the diner and you know how dangerous that can be." She rolled her eyes. "Bring Sophie over for lunch and I'll get the particulars of the case then." Holly turned her attention back to Sophie. "We can talk while you eat. After lunch, Cain can run you home. We'll be sure to get your car back to you first thing in the morning." With a wave over her shoulder, she hurried out.

Both of them stared at the empty doorway and then Sophie asked, "Is it just me or does it feel like she sucked all the energy out of the room when she left? Is she always so bubbly and energetic?"

"Bubbly and energetic?" Cain grinned. "Those aren't the words I'd use to describe Holly. More like impish, meddlesome and a royal pain at times. But I love her."

Cain's expression sobered. He tilted Sophie's chin and examined the bruise on her cheek. "How are you doing?"

"Fine. Except for a headache. Probably from all the excitement." She gingerly placed her fingers to her scalp. "Thanks to you, I barely hit anything. And even if I had, my dad always said I'm hardheaded."

She made a point of studying Cain. "What about you? I'm not the only one who took a nasty spill. Were you hurt?"

Cain moved his right hand and Sophie could see a bandage stretching from the tip of his little finger to his wrist. She sucked in a breath. "Ouch, you were hurt."

"This?" Cain shrugged, dismissing it as insignificant.

"This isn't anything. But tomorrow I bet we're both going to be sore in spots we didn't even know we had."

Sophie's stomach growled again.

Cain laughed out loud. "Let me lock up and I'll take you for that lunch I promised."

He put the first aid kit away, made sure the coffeepot was unplugged and gently followed her into the hall. Sliding his key into the lock, he glanced at her.

"Sophie, what happened this afternoon was not an accident. Someone deliberately tried to run you down."

She shook her head. "No way. It was probably an older person who got their foot caught on the accelerator. Or a teenager texting. Or whatever."

"Sophie." His grim expression and the way he dragged out the syllables in her name told her he wasn't buying her explanations.

Dread oozed up her spine. First her father disappeared. Then she found out his identification papers were fake—then hers turned out to be phony, too. Now this. Sophie didn't have a clue what was going on but none of it felt good.

"I'm not trying to frighten you," Cain said and walked with her outside.

Really? You're doing a pretty good job of it.

"I saw a man dash for his car when he saw you. He accelerated when you stepped into the street. There was nothing random or accidental about it."

Maybe if she closed her eyes really tight she'd wake up and find out this had been a terrible nightmare. Sophie squeezed her eyes shut, counted to five and then slowly opened them. Nope. Still Main Street. Still Cain standing there with that worried look on his face. She hadn't been dreaming. But, boy, she wished she had.

"Your father's letter said he left to keep you safe." The soft, low tenor of Cain's voice soothed her. "But I bet you don't feel very safe these days, do you? Something is happening and I want to help you get to the bottom of it."

She locked eyes with him. "You've changed your mind? You're going to help me?"

Cain grinned. "I never said I wasn't going to help you. I said that I didn't think I *could* help you. Face it, you haven't given me a lot to go on. But I never said I wouldn't try."

Sophie nodded and hung her head.

He gave her hand a quick, reassuring squeeze and her heart skipped a beat. Why'd he have to be so kind? It didn't hurt that he was good-looking, too. How was she supposed to think straight if her heart took silly little jumps every time he looked her way?

"Considering what happened today, we're going to have to try harder to find a place to start looking." Cain glanced up and down the street. "Your father was right, Sophie. You're in danger. The question is, why?"

THREE

The diner looked like something right out of a 1950s magazine, black-and-white tile floor, red vinyl booths, red covered stools at the counter and polished chrome everywhere. Small jukeboxes graced the tables and stood at attention at marked intervals along the speckled counter top. The steady hum of quiet conversations mingled in the air with competing strands of music from the jukeboxes. Sophie paused for a moment and looked around. It must be close to lunchtime. The place was packed. As the tantalizing aroma of home cooking wafted in the air, she knew why. Her mouth watered like she was a participant in a Pavlov experiment.

"Over here," Holly yelled, waving them to the counter. "I've saved a couple of seats. We can talk while you eat."

Sophie weaved her way through several people waiting for seats. Normally, she would have been kinder and waited her turn in line but not today. Today it was every man—or woman, as the case may be—for themselves. She hadn't eaten since lunchtime yesterday. One glance at the huge burgers and home-cut fries at the booth beside her gave her the incentive to move faster as she whispered, "Sorry," and elbowed her way to the counter. She plopped down on the stool Holly had reserved for her. Seconds later Cain slid in beside her.

"Wow! This place really does a business." Sophie glanced around the crowded diner and smiled at Holly.

"Some people say we're packed because the food is fantastic. Others say it's because we're the only diner in town." Holly laughed. "I don't care what the reason. I'm just happy they come. Now, what can I get for you?"

"I'll take a burger and fries," Sophie replied. "With lettuce, tomato and onion."

"And to drink?"

Before she could answer, Cain said, "I'll order the same and you can bring us a couple of large chocolate shakes." When Holly hurried away, he leaned his elbow on the counter and swung to face her. "This diner has the best chocolate shakes—and the best charbroiled burgers—and on Tuesdays we serve fabulous pot roast dinners…"

"And apple pie. Don't forget you told me this place serves the best apple pie."

Cain laughed. "Okay, I admit I probably sound like a bad advertisement for fast food. But I dare you to finish your meal and not smack your lips."

Sophie grinned. "No way. I'm not stupid. I looked at the food on the way in and I'm not taking that bet. Those burgers are so thick I'm wondering how I'm going to open my mouth wide enough to take a bite."

"Believe me, you'll find a way."

Holly placed two glasses of water and silverware in front of them and disappeared again before Sophie could do more than blink.

Cain leaned closer so he could be heard above the hum of other conversations and the beats of music. "I've been thinking about your situation. There's got to be something you're overlooking. An old letter. Something in the background of a picture. A name. Date. Something."

Sophie shrugged. "I can't imagine what it would be. I've

spent the past two weeks searching for clues and I keep coming up empty."

Cain reached over and brushed a strand of hair from her face.

When his fingertips slid across her skin, her heart pounded so hard she thought it would leap right out of her chest. She sat perfectly still, not daring to break the welcome contact or even to breathe.

"This has been a tough day for you." His eyes looked like pools of dark chocolate and all Sophie could think about was how much she liked desserts.

"Coming through. Hot stuff here." Holly slid two platters overflowing with food in front of them. "Let the girl get some food in her empty stomach, Romeo. Make your moves later."

Cain's expression darkened like an incoming storm. "You can be a real pain. You know that?"

Holly grinned. "What's a kid sister for? Be back in a sec with your shakes."

Sophie blinked in surprise when Cain clasped her hand, bowed his head and offered a quiet blessing. When he looked up, he grinned and said, "Go ahead. Dig in. And tell me if you don't think that's the best burger you've ever tasted."

Sophie didn't need a second invitation.

They sat in companionable silence enjoying their meal.

A short while later Sophie pushed back her empty platter and patted her stomach. "I can't believe I ate the whole thing. I'm so stuffed I can hardly breathe."

"And?" he prompted.

"And I have to admit it was the best burger I've ever eaten."

Cain laughed. "Told you so."

Holly cleared the dirty dishes and was back in a flash. She propped her elbows on the counter and said, "So, spill. I want to hear every nasty detail. Girl, what have you done to get someone mad enough to try and run you down?"

Cain and Sophie took turns filling her in on the little information they had.

"Wow," Holly said when they'd finished bringing her up to date. "I don't know what's spookier—not knowing what happened to your dad—or waking up one morning not knowing who you are."

Sophie grimaced. Holly had honed in on exactly what was eating her up inside. It was bad enough she didn't know what had happened to her father. But her father was strong, sensible. She had faith that he'd be able to take care of himself.

But, as for the rest...

How could she explain how it felt to have spent twenty-two years believing you were one person only to find out you were somebody else? Worse. Not knowing who that somebody else was? Was Sophie even her name? Maybe she was Carol or Jennifer or maybe Nancy. She played with the names in her mind. None of them felt like a fit.

And what if her father wasn't even her father? After all, his papers were fake. Maybe he was a fake. Maybe they weren't related at all.

A wave of pain washed over her. No. He was her father. He had to be her father. She wouldn't be able to love him so deeply, miss him so terribly if he weren't her father, would she?

Where was he?

Sophie agonized over the events of the past two weeks. Question after question and not one single answer. She felt like she was starring in a science fiction movie. And she hated science fiction. Any second now she expected to stand in front of a mirror and see a different face—a different woman—an image she'd never seen before.

"Sophie?"

The deep, resonant sound of Cain's voice pulled her thoughts back to the present.

"You okay?" Lines of concern creased his brow and drew deep frown lines at the edges of his mouth.

"Sure." She smiled at both Cain and Holly. "Lunch was great. Thanks." Cain raised an eyebrow and Sophie laughed. "Okay, it was more than great. It was the best!" The three of them chuckled. "But I really should be getting home."

Before Sophie could rise someone jostled her elbow. "Hi, little lady." Sophie turned her attention to the grizzled, disheveled man standing at her left elbow. "You must be new in town. I'll admit I'm gettin' up in years but these here eyes of mine still appreciate the sight of a pretty gal when I see one. And I'm seeing one now."

"Hey, Charlie," Holly said

"Charlie." Cain nodded in the old man's direction. His tone had been polite but Sophie couldn't help but notice a subtle tensing of his posture. She sensed Cain wasn't very fond of good old Charlie.

Sophie looked into pale, watery-blue eyes peeking out from beneath bushy white brows. His skin, leathered from weather and age, looked almost reptilian. His teeth, what few he still had, were yellow and stained, from years of tobacco use, Sophie suspected—smoking or chewing she couldn't be sure.

"So introduce yourself, little lady. I know I haven't seen you around town."

"My name's Sophie."

"That right?" He swayed back and forth, rocking on the heels of old, worn boots. "Just passing through or planning to stay awhile?"

The strong scent of alcohol wafted her way and Sophie began to feel uncomfortable.

"I…I'm planning on staying…for a little while anyway."

Sophie smiled at the old man and tried to subtly move out of the line of alcohol breath.

"Charlie, you met the young lady. Now why don't you sit down over there and Holly will bring you a cup of coffee?"

Charlie ignored Cain. "You wouldn't be the gal I heard is staying in the old Weatherly place, would ya?"

Sophie nodded. "Yes. The cottage belonged to my grandfather and I'll be staying there for a little while."

Charlie's whole demeanor changed. Instead of the overly friendly, tipsy man she'd been talking to just moments before, she found herself staring into cold, angry eyes.

"You tellin' me you're Elizabeth Weatherly's young'un?"

Sophie, surprised by the abrupt and hostile change in the man's demeanor, merely nodded.

"Your grandfather was a friend of mine. My best friend. We used to go fishin' out at the old pond all the time." The man stepped closer.

Cain sprang to his feet. "C'mon, Charlie. Go sit down and have some coffee. I'll even throw in a slice of Holly's apple pie...on me. What do you say?"

Spittle ran down the man's whiskered chin as he spat out his words. "Your mama broke my friend's heart. He was never the same after she run off. Never."

Cain stepped between the two of them. "Charlie, don't make me have to ask you to leave. Go sit down. Now." His lowered voice and stern, no-nonsense tone brought chills up on her arms. She had a glimpse of what Cain must have been like when he was a cop, and she was glad she wasn't a criminal on the receiving end of his wrath. Silence fell over the diner as the other patrons watched the scene unfolding before them.

"Do you know who this is?" Charlie yelled, flailing his arms and looking around at the people in the surrounding booths. "This is George Weatherly's no-good kin. The daughter of the brat who ran off and broke his heart."

"That's it. You're out of here." Cain grabbed the man's belt and heaved him toward the exit.

"We don't want your kind in this town, missy," he yelled as Cain lifted him through the doorway. "You hear me? We don't want you in our town."

Sophie couldn't believe what had just happened. Her cheeks burned with embarrassment as she shot furtive glances around the room and saw people staring at her and whispering.

"Don't worry about old Charlie." Holly patted her hand. "Every town has its drunk and Charlie's ours. Don't pay attention to anything he says."

Sophie glanced from side to side. Whenever she made eye contact with the other diners, the people looked away. She didn't really understand what had just happened. She only knew that the entire incident made her feel embarrassed, ashamed and dirty.

She buried her head in her hands. How could this day get any worse?

A strong hand cupped her shoulder. "You've had enough excitement for one day. Why don't I take you home?"

Emptiness filled her insides when his hand moved away. She longed for the comfort. She longed for someone to hold her and tell her that all this craziness would disappear and everything would soon be back to normal. If anything would ever be normal again.

"We'll sit down tomorrow morning," Cain said as he led her to his car, "after you've had a good night's sleep, and we'll talk it all out."

Sophie was amazed at how easy and comfortable she felt with this man.

Maybe he'd be able to help her after all. Her father had taught her God never closes a door without opening another one. Sophie had prayed so hard for someone to help her find her father, to help her solve the puzzle of his disappearance and maybe even discover her true identity. Was Cain an answer to her prayers?

She stared at his profile, the firm set to his jaw, the perfect line of his nose. A hunk of errant hair refused to stay in place and fell on his forehead, drawing attention to his newly blackened eye, which came from his earlier superhero rescue. This morning he had been nothing more than a name in a church business directory. This afternoon he was not only the man who had saved her life but a man who was quickly becoming a friend.

The miles flew by and Sophie was surprised when the car pulled to a stop. Cain shut the engine off, hurried around and opened her door. She tried not to laugh. When was the last time anyone had held a car door open for her? Duh, never.

"Thanks for everything, Cain." She climbed out and smiled up at him, the door between the two of them. "Just the thought of what could have happened to me today if you hadn't done what you did…"

"Glad I could help."

When he started up the sidewalk with her, she said, "You don't have to come in. I'm fine. I know you have to get back to your office."

"Trying to get rid of me, are you?" His eyes twinkled with amusement. "I'm not leaving until I'm sure you're safely inside."

Sophie preceded him up the sidewalk to the small but picturesque cottage and drew in a sharp breath. The door was standing ajar.

FOUR

The flashing strobe lights of the police vehicles pulsated through the curtains and danced along the walls of the room. The sheriff and other officers strode through each room as though they thought it was a public arena instead of the private confines of her home. Sophie never knew you could feel violated by both the criminals who ransacked through your personal belongings as well as the police officers who went through the same belongings, taking pictures and dusting for prints.

She kept in the background and waited. Waited for the techs to finish gathering their evidence. Waited for the police to finish their reports. Waited for the reality of the broken and strewn pieces of her life to sink through the fog that enveloped her. Why was all of this happening? Each minute this living nightmare worsened.

A shadow fell across her lap. Sophie looked up, stretching her head back so she could look into the eyes of the large, solidly built man looming over her.

"Ms. Clarkston." He tipped his hat. "I didn't expect to be seeing you again so soon."

"Ditto on that one, Sheriff."

"I need to ask you a few questions. Are you comfortable here or would you like to move into the kitchen?"

"Here's fine." She unwrapped her legs and scooted over to make room for him on the sofa. The sheriff remained standing.

"I make it my business to know the people in this town, Ms. Clarkston. How come I don't know you…other than from the episode earlier today with that hit-and-run?"

She glanced into the man's hard, steely gaze and felt like she'd just been slapped. "I…I don't know, Sheriff. I've only been in town a couple of weeks. I guess our paths just haven't crossed."

"Is this your house, ma'am?"

Sophie nodded.

"To my knowledge, no one's lived in this place for years."

Sophie squirmed beneath the accusatory tone in the man's voice. "My father and I don't come here very often. Maybe once or twice a year. My father pays someone to keep an eye on the place and keep it cleaned and stocked since we never know when we'll be coming home."

"Home?" The sheriff removed his hat and ran a hand through his thin, graying hair. "To my recollection this cottage belongs to the Weatherly family. Christopher Weatherly was one of the original founders of our town. Back in the late eighteen hundreds, I believe. And his family have been pillars of our community ever since." He put his hat back on his head. "So pardon me, ma'am, if I find it right peculiar that all of a sudden there's a young lady living in this residence. Your name's not Weatherly, now, is it?"

Sophie's stomach cramped with anxiety. How was she going to explain this to the sheriff? She didn't have any papers to prove this was her home, only a key. And when she told him her name…or at least the name she had always believed was her name…he'd run a check, if he hadn't already, and he'd find out her entire life as she knew it was all a lie. Hot tears threatened to spill from her eyes, but a stubbornness she knew she'd inherited from her father refused to let them fall. She would not show weakness or defeat in front of this sheriff—or anyone else.

"Elizabeth Weatherly was my mother, Sheriff. I believe that counts for being a member of the Weatherly family."

The sheriff's mouth opened. "Little Elizabeth Weatherly? She's your mama?" The sheriff studied her intently. "Of course, I see the resemblance now. I didn't notice it sooner because I haven't seen Elizabeth since high school."

A smile split his face. "Where's your mama now? I can't wait to catch up on old times. Don't worry. We'll have this property ownership thing cleared up just as soon as I talk with your mama."

Sophie had a difficult time remaining patient. Why wasn't the sheriff out chasing the bad guys instead of wasting precious time worrying about her right to be in her own home? "That's going to be a little difficult, Sheriff. My mother died shortly after my birth."

The sheriff threw back his shoulders, straightened to his full height and stared back at her.

"That so?"

Sophie nodded.

"Well, that's too bad. I would have enjoyed speaking with her again after all these years. If I remember correctly, she left shortly after graduation. Ran off with some fellow her granddaddy was gunning for and no one's seen or heard from her since." He scratched the gray stubble on his chin and stared hard at her. "I have to admit you're as pretty as your mama was."

He plopped his hat back on his head. "I'll check with the title company and see if the cottage is in your mama's name or if your grandfather sold it off after she left town. Cain Garrison over there said your name is Sophie Joy Clarkston. Give me your daddy's full name and where he's staying. I'd like to talk to him. As soon as he produces a marriage license, that's all the proof I need that this place belongs to you."

Sophie's stomach turned over and bile clung to the back of her throat but she fought hard not to show any outward signs of turmoil in front of the sheriff. "Don't you have your priorities a little out of order, Sheriff?" Although she kept her tone of voice light and ladylike, there was no mistaking the hostility in it. "Shouldn't you and your men be concentrating on finding the people who broke into my home, instead of worrying about real estate titles and marriage licenses?"

The sheriff's eyes narrowed. "Oh, you can rest assured, little lady, I'll find the person who trashed this house and at the same time I'll find out if this is your home in the first place." He placed his hand on his belt, thrumming his fingers against the butt of his gun. "Meanwhile I'd try to keep a low profile if I were you. You've already caused enough excitement in this town with your near hit-and-run. Now this. If the incident at the diner this afternoon wasn't enough to clue you in, let me remind you that your grandfather was a highly respected and loved member of our community."

Sophie blinked hard but remained silent. She shouldn't be surprised that the sheriff had already heard about the altercation with Charlie in Holly's diner. Gossip in a small town travels faster than a brush fire after a drought.

"A lot of folks won't be happy to know Elizabeth Weatherly's daughter is back in town," the sheriff said. "The memory of your granddaddy's broken heart is still fresh in most people's minds."

He stared hard at her as if he was waiting for his words to have an impact. "So I'll hop to it, ma'am, and get started on investigating the bad guy who trashed your place." His eyes narrowed . "But I'm also gonna make a point of talking with your daddy about the title and marriage license, too. No sense leaving any questions unanswered now is there, ma'am?" He tipped his hat in a "have a good day gesture" and walked away.

Sophie's legs trembled, refusing to hold her upright a moment longer. She plopped down on the edge of the sofa and drew in a deep breath. What would the sheriff do when he found out her identity was a fake and her father was missing? Would he throw her out in the street? Where would she go? What would happen to her then? She lowered her face in her hands. More importantly, where was her father? He held all the answers to her questions. Was he dead or alive? She had to know his whereabouts. Even if he was dead, she had to know. Not knowing was its own kind of nightmare.

She looked up and her eyes scanned the room. Who had done this to her home? What did they want? Had they found what they came for or would they be back to search some more? Fear crept down her spine.

Sophie's father had gone out of his way to teach her to be strong and independent. Considering the events of the past two weeks, she felt like he had been training her for this very day. But the past two weeks had taken their toll. She'd lost her father…twice. She was still reeling from both his disappearance and his deception. As if that hadn't been enough, someone had tried to run her down today. And now her home had been ransacked.

Was it so wrong to need someone to talk to? Someone to help her make sense out of the chaos? She lowered her head and wished she was still on speaking terms with God.

When she looked up again, her eyes locked with Cain's across the room. Within seconds, he excused himself from his conversation with one of the officers and headed her way. Her heart skipped a beat and a rush of heat filled her cheeks. Was she that transparent? Could a mere glance communicate her confusion, her fear…her need for comfort?

* * *

Cain had seen a flash of panic in Sophie's eyes. But that's all it had been. A flash. A split second of letting down her guard before she returned to wearing her protective mask of self-reliance and strength. His heart filled with empathy.

He stepped gingerly over the broken items strewn on the floor and made his way across the living room. So much had happened to her in such a short period of time. She was holding up a lot better than most folks would in her situation. Probably better than he would if he had to face the loss of his dad and the fallout from a lifetime of deception. But she was hanging in there. He had to admit he admired her.

Then he reminded himself that he shouldn't be feeling admiration or empathy, or anything else for that matter. This was a job. Sophie was nothing more than a client in trouble and needing his professional help. *Professional help, buddy. Keep your emotions out of it. No matter how cute she is. No matter how vulnerable beneath that tough persona. That's your Achilles' heel, remember? Your fatal flaw, to always want to run to the rescue. Not this time. Professionalism all the way.*

Cain sat beside her. "It's going to be okay." Sophie lifted her eyes to his. He smiled to offer reassurance and perhaps a *little* comfort. "Have you had a chance to look around? Is anything missing?"

Sophie sighed and forced herself to take another look around the room. Drawers hung open, their contents scattered across the gray carpeting. Pictures hung askew on the walls or had been pulled down and the frames shattered. Clutter and chaos flowed in one unbroken rhythm from the living room to the kitchen, and she imagined it continued into the bedrooms. She hadn't had the heart to walk back there yet and see.

"It's hard to tell," she replied. "Everything's been moved... and broken...and..." Her voice choked on a sob. "I'm sorry."

"Don't be," Cain said. "You're doing fine. You've been through a lot today."

Sophie squinted at something she saw in the distance. She jumped up, hurried across the room and carefully lifted a wooden box lying open on the floor.

Cain came up behind her. "Is it broken?"

She turned the small chest around, examining it for damage, and then clasped it against her chest.

"No." A look of relief flooded her face.

"It's special?"

Sophie lowered the small box and ran her fingers slowly, almost tenderly, across the hand-carved design on the lid. "My dad made this for me when I was just a kid." Tears shimmered in her eyes but she blinked them back and forced a smile. "My father is a craftsman, loves woodworking." She swept her hand in a slow arc around the room. "Almost everything in here...the furniture, cabinets...even the picture frames were all hand-carved by my dad." Her smile was bittersweet. "He loves working with his hands. He has a true gift for carving."

"Is that how he made his living? The Charlottesville police report couldn't find any tax returns or bank accounts in his name." As soon as the words were out of his mouth, he wished he could call them back. She stiffened and the smile faded from her lips. The questions had to be asked. But did he have to ask them right now?

He felt her eyes on him, studying him, choosing her words before answering. "My dad's an artist. He hand carves furniture, animal lawn ornaments, unique wooden birdhouses, all sorts of things. He'd travel across the country from one craft fair to another selling his wares."

"You traveled with him?"

She blinked with surprise and then grinned. "Of course. I literally grew up on the craft circuit. We'd frequent many of the larger annual fairs. After a couple of years, it was like a family reunion meeting up again with the friends we knew from the years before."

Cain took the box from her hands and studied the intricate design carved into the lid. "This is beautiful."

Sophie beamed with pride. "Thank you."

He handed it back. "What about school?"

"I was homeschooled. Dad used to say I'd get more of an education touring the United States than I would ever get in an overcrowded classroom."

Cain digested the information and wondered if he should take a chance and push for more. Treading as carefully as he could, he asked, "Have you always traveled with your dad? I understand you had to when you were a kid. But you're not a kid anymore, Sophie. Did you ever want to do something else? Something on your own, maybe?"

Sophie shrugged. "Sure. Doesn't every teenager long for the day they can leave home and set out on their own? I wasn't any different."

Cain gave her a questioning look but remained silent.

"Around my eighteenth birthday, my dad got sick. We thought he'd had a heart attack but it was just a really bad respiratory infection causing muscle spasms in his chest. But it scared me silly. Dad had never been sick before. I realized not only was he the only family I had, I was the only family he had, too. It had been the two of us for so many years and if I left—"

She stared off into space, lost in thoughts of long ago.

"I couldn't leave. He needed me. Besides, I did do something on my own." Her smile widened and it lit up her face. "I became an artist myself."

"Wood carving?" Cain couldn't keep the surprise out of his voice.

Sophie shook her head. "No. When I was little, I used to try and make things out of mud pies. Dad sensed I had a drop of creativity of my own. He surprised me with clay and a small kiln."

"You sculpt?"

Sophie nodded. "Don't look so surprised."

"I'm not…I mean, I am but…"

"Remind me to show you some of my work. Maybe I'll even let you try it sometime. There's something awesome about feeling a slab of clay ooze through your fingers. Kneading it. Molding it into something unique and beautiful."

Unique and beautiful.

His thoughts exactly as he stared into her upturned face.

"Sometimes I think God gifts the sculptor with just a tiny bit of insight into what it must have been like for Him when He created us out of dust," Sophie said.

"I thought you didn't believe in God." Cain grinned at her.

"I believe in God. I'm just not on speaking terms with Him right now."

"Really? Do you think that's wise? Who shut the door? You or Him?"

Sophie chewed on her lower lip and lowered her head.

Not wanting her to slip back into a morose mood, Cain gripped her elbow and steered her toward the kitchen. "C'mon, let me help you clean up this mess. Find me a broom and I'll sweep up. But don't you dare tell Holly I had anything to do with housework. She's been after me for years to clean up after myself at the house, and I'll never hear the end of it if she learns I actually know how to use a broom."

Cain followed Sophie from room to room as she surveyed the damage to her home and belongings. Her shoulders sagged and each step seemed difficult for her. But she didn't cry anymore.

Thank you, Lord, for small favors. You know how a woman's tears make me feel so helpless. And that leads to bad decisions. Fatal decisions.

They had just come down the short hall when the sheriff stepped into their path.

"Ms. Clarkston, I'm fixin' to head out. We've done all we can do for now."

Sophie wrapped her arms around herself and nodded. She looked pitiful. Fragile. Defeated. Alone. A man's heart would have to be made of ice-cold steel not to be moved. Apparently, the sheriff agreed with Cain's line of thought. He placed a comforting hand on Sophie's arms and his voice softened. "This is a lousy way to welcome you to Promise, Ms. Clarkston. And I'm really sorry that you have to suffer through it."

He stepped back and straightened his hat. "I'm planning on getting to the bottom of this, ma'am. You can count on it. And as soon as I get the chance to talk to your daddy, I'm sure we'll be able to clear up some of the misunderstandings."

Sophie's shoulders stiffened. She offered a weak smile, nodded but remained silent.

"Meanwhile, I'm leaving you in good hands." The sheriff gestured to Cain. "I'm sure he plans to stay here and help you clean up this mess. Isn't that right, son?"

Cain smiled. *Son.* He hadn't been called that since his grammar school days. "Don't worry, Sheriff. I'm on it."

The sheriff nodded, signaled to his men and they left.

Sophie didn't release a breath until she saw their cars disappear down the dirt road, spewing a cloud of dust.

"What's going to happen when the sheriff discovers my dad's information is fake?" she asked in a soft, unsteady voice.

"I imagine he'll come back with a lot more questions." Cain lifted her chin with his finger and gazed into her turbulent green eyes. "But since you don't know any more than he does, you have nothing to be afraid of."

"Right." Sophie offered a tentative smile. "I didn't do anything wrong and I don't have anything to worry about, do I?"

"I wouldn't go that far. You don't have anything to worry about from the sheriff." Cain gestured around the living room. "But someone is going to a lot of trouble to make sure you worry about them."

FIVE

Two hours later, Cain tied up the last of the trash bags and hauled them out to the shed. He could see Sophie leaning in the doorway, her arms folded across her chest, waiting for him to return. When he approached he noted a purplish hue shadowing the tender skin beneath her eyes and a deep sadness radiating from within her. The tears she'd fought hard to hold at bay all day slowly flowed down her cheeks. She straightened and her arms fell to her sides.

"Why is this happening, Cain? I can't make any sense of it. Dad and I lived a quiet life. Minded our own business. I don't understand why anyone would want to harm us." She clamped her teeth together and swiped the tears from her cheeks. "I need to know what happened to him. And I plan to find out."

Cain gazed at the petite five-foot-two bundle of resolve standing in front of him and he didn't know how to keep his heart encased in steel—only that he would, he had to, no matter what. He couldn't afford to make a second mistake. He'd paid too high a price for the last one. A wave of pain squeezed his heart at the memories and, rather than try to push them back into the closed little closets he'd created in his mind, he embraced the pain. The pain was good. The pain would help him erect a wall—and keep it there.

His gaze traveled up and down the length of her. Way out of her element, looking bewildered, afraid, still Sophie stood there, shoulders back, head held high, and threw down the gauntlet for him to step up and help or get out of her way. He smiled and shook his head. *Of course he was going to help. As soon as he figured out how to find a ghost.*

"Relax, Sophie. I told you I'd help and I will."

He rested his head back against the porch column and took a few minutes to enjoy the impending sunset. The sun hung low in the sky. Brilliant colors of pink, lavender, blue and purple swirled across the sky. He wasn't sure which was God's most artistic masterpiece, the breathtaking sunset or the silhouette of Sophie standing on the top step of the porch.

"I wish you'd come into town with me." He tried to keep his apprehension out of his voice. The last thing she needed was more stress today. But it didn't feel right leaving her out here surrounded by woods and all alone.

"Don't be silly," Sophie said. "This is my home."

"I know but…"

"No buts. The people who tossed my house are probably as dog tired as I am. They're not planning on coming back tonight." She smiled up at him. "Now, go. Seriously. Before it gets much later."

He straightened but didn't move off the porch.

"Cain, really, I appreciate you worrying about me. I truly do. But I'll be fine. I'll go inside and lock the doors and the windows the second you leave. Besides, your hourly rate and my budget aren't that compatible." She grinned the second he started to protest and then he realized she was teasing him about owing him money. She knew he wouldn't think of charging her for this and had gotten the rise out of him she'd expected.

He grinned in return. "A man knows when he's been defeated." He bowed his head and then lumbered down the steps. He opened the driver's door and paused before slipping inside. "Lock up. Immediately."

Sophie stood and saluted. "Yes, sir."

Cain shook his head, slid behind the wheel and started the engine.

She watched the tail end of his compact car disappear down the dirt road. A grin twisted her lips. From the size of the dust cloud behind him, it was obvious his foot leaned heavily on the accelerator. For a man who hadn't wanted to leave he sure was in a hurry now.

Sophie started to go inside but decided to steal a moment—just one, quiet, uneventful moment—and enjoy the twilight. She wrapped an arm around the porch post and stared into the distance. This was exactly the kind of night her father and she would have spent together. They'd have worked on their separate projects most of the day, come together for dinner, and then carried a final cup of coffee out on the porch to sit, talk, just be together.

Her throat closed up. *Oh, Daddy, how could you do this?* Instantly her mind jumped to thoughts she didn't want to have and taunted her with them. *Are you sure he's your father? How do you know? You don't even know his real name. How can you be sure of anything anymore?* The emotional pain that swept from head to toe couldn't have hurt more if she was being physically tortured.

She had lived her entire life believing she was Sophia Joy Clarkston. Sophie—the person who loved strawberries and thick cream. Who loved walking barefoot in sand. Who loved the change of colors in the fall, the smell of lilacs in spring and the scent of pine at Christmas. The same Sophie who loved to mold and create objects, animals and people out of a shapeless lump of clay. The Sophie who cherished the opportunities to sit on a porch swing or lie in the grass and count the stars.

If she wasn't really Sophia Joy Clarkston, then who was she? And did everything she remembered, everything she'd done, everything she'd ever believed she was, now suddenly change because she wasn't the person she'd thought she was?

A tear slipped down her cheek.

Oh, Dad! What were you thinking? Why didn't you talk to me...trust me?

Over the years, she'd met many older people at the craft fairs that wished they could live their lives over. Start fresh with a clean slate. But Sophie wondered, if they were given that option, if everything they thought they were was gone and they had nothing—no family, no expectations, no memories—would they want their life erased as simply as chalk off a blackboard? She didn't. At least she knew that much about herself—no matter who or what her *real* name would turn out to be.

A sudden chill skittered along her nerve endings. Sophie hugged herself and quietly scanned the trees. She didn't see anything out of the ordinary. No lurking figures in the bushes. No threatening shadows. Her ears strained to listen for any unusual or stealth-like sounds. All she heard was the cacophony of crickets and frogs mingling with the normal rustling of nocturnal animals coming awake and moving around in the brush.

Still. She scanned her surroundings again—slowly, searching, lingering on every leaf, bush and stone. She found nothing threatening. Nothing scary. So why did her instincts tell her she was being watched? She didn't have the answer but she trusted her instincts.

She hurried inside and threw the dead bolt behind her. She locked each window in the house for good measure.

She had just finished dressing after her shower and was towel drying her hair when she heard a knock at the door. *Cain*. A grin pulled at the corners of her mouth. Although he'd promised to bring her car out to her in the morning, from the way he sped out of here she'd had the feeling he would be back. She tossed the towel in the hamper, took one quick look at her reflection in the mirror, smoothed her hair and hurried toward the front door. She opened it just as Cain lifted his hand to knock again.

"You didn't check." He frowned.

"What?" Sophie blinked hard.

Cain slipped past her with Holly close behind and they both turned to face her. "You didn't look out the window to see who was here. You just opened the door."

"Oh, come on…" Sophie shut the door.

"I don't side with my brother often." Holly sat down on the nearest chair. "But this time he's right, kiddo. You should have checked before you opened the door. You didn't know for sure it was us."

"Let me get this straight. You're saying if the robber comes back, he's going to knock on the door and announce himself first. Who is crazier, you or me?"

Both Garrisons crossed their arms and stared at her in silence.

"Okay." Sophie laughed and threw her arms up in surrender. "You win. I should have checked before I opened the door."

Cain gave a sigh of relief. "Okay, now that that's out of the way, Holly has agreed to stay with you tonight."

Sophie glanced at the small overnight bag at Holly's feet and groaned. She'd already learned arguing with Cain was a losing battle, so she stated her case directly to Holly.

"I appreciate the offer, Holly. It could be fun. It would give us a chance to get to know each other better, and you could catch me up on all the town gossip."

Holly laughed. "That could keep us up all night. Small towns are what originated soap operas, you know."

Sophie smiled. "But not tonight."

Holly blinked and Cain's frown deepened.

Sophie raised a hand to stop them before they said a word. "It's been a long and very stressful day. All I want is to forget today ever happened, climb into bed with a good book and then get a good night's sleep."

"But…"

"No buts, Cain." Sophie stood her ground. "Holly, thank you so much for driving my car out here. I know you must be tired after working in the diner and I really appreciate it." She placed her hand lightly on Cain's forearm. "And, Cain, I know those ex-police officer genes of yours are chomping at the bit to catch this bad guy. I get it. I do."

She locked eyes with his and tried to ignore the butterflies batting around in her stomach. "I honestly don't believe this person would be stupid enough to try and come back on the same night."

Cain opened his mouth to reply and again she stopped him.

"But if he is stupid enough to try again, I have 911 on speed dial, my bedroom door locks and I will even hide my video camera next to the fern on the mantel above the fireplace. This way if someone does break in he'll be caught red-handed while you are busy racing to my rescue, because *I* will be safely barricaded in my room and will have already called 911, the sheriff and you."

Holly grinned. "A gal after my own heart, bro. She's one strong, independent lady."

Cain glowered at his sister. "Who are you helping?"

"Me," Sophie said. She removed her hand from his arm

and smiled up at him. "Both of you are helping *me*. I'm so grateful for making such good friends so quickly." Slowly, she opened the front door. "But the best way you can help me right now is to go home. I need to get a good night's sleep. So do you. Tomorrow is another day."

Cain muttered under his breath and stepped onto the porch. Holly patted Sophie's hand as she stepped past her and whispered, "You go, girl," under her breath.

Sophie accepted her car keys from Holly.

"Thanks, again."

"Don't mention it." Holly skipped down the steps and climbed in the passenger seat of her brother's car.

Cain put his hands on his hips. "If it wasn't so deserted out here—"

"Cain." She waited until they made eye contact and she knew she had his undivided attention. "This is my *home*. The only one I have. Please don't try to make me scared to be in it. I'll be fine. Now, go." She gestured him off the porch.

"Are you coming into town tomorrow?"

"You bet. You and I have work to do. We have to try and locate my father before the sheriff discovers he's missing in action, so to speak."

Cain frowned again. "I wouldn't count on us beating the sheriff."

Sophie swung her shoulders back. "I know you just met me. But in case you haven't noticed, Mr. Cain Garrison, I don't scare easily. I don't back down. And I am determined to find out what happened to my dad. The way I figure it, you can spend the morning on your computer, seeing if you can prove this house belongs to me and whatever else you can find. As for me—"

She glanced behind her. "The jerk came here looking for something. My gut says he didn't find it. But I will. There's got to be something in this place that will help us find the answers we need."

Sophie turned back to Cain. "What's that old cliché? Hell hath no fury like a woman scorned? Well, I'm furious, Cain. I'm going to find out the truth—no matter where it leads."

Cain grinned, a slow, lazy, tantalizing grin and Sophie all but melted into the floorboards.

"You're a mass of contradictions, Sophie. You're young. Naive in some ways. Fragile." He held his hand up to stop her protests. "Yet you remind me of that complimentary term used for southern women who are soft and cuddly on the outside but iron inside. I think they call them steel magnolias, don't they?" He tweaked the bottom of her chin. "Okay, you win. I'll do one quick turn around the outside of the house to make sure everything's locked up tight and then I'll see you tomorrow."

It was the wee small hours of the morning when Cain returned to the cottage. Headlights off and driving as noise-lessly as possible, he eased his car up the dirt road. He stopped about a hundred yards from the house and turned off the engine. His eyes strained to scan the yard leading into the woods. When he didn't see anything out of the ordinary, he turned his attention to the house.

A single light shone from a back window. He knew from having been inside earlier that it was coming from one of the bedrooms. He couldn't believe Sophie was still up. She had to be exhausted after the day she'd had. He sat in silence, patiently waiting for the light to go out. Thirty minutes later it did.

With a sigh of relief, Cain adjusted a pillow against a window and tried to stretch his legs out in the passenger well. He knew he was in for a long, uncomfortable night. But if the mountain wouldn't come to him, then he'd have to go to the mountain. Sometimes he wished the Lord would take away his damsels-in-distress Achilles' heel. Then again, he glanced back at the darkened house. Sometimes he was glad He didn't.

SIX

Tap. Tap. Tap.

Cain awoke with a start. What? Where? He must have drifted off. The sun shone brightly in his face and he threw up a hand to shield his eyes.

Tap. Tap. Tap. The sound was louder this time.

He turned his head. A figure blocked out the sun, the solid dark outline surrounded by sunlight preventing him from identifying the person outside his car window. Swiftly, Cain sat up, stifling a groan at the pain that shot up his leg when he pulled it beneath him. He tried to shake off the sleepy fog enveloping his mind like a warm blanket.

He wasn't so lethargic, however, that he'd act foolishly. One hand surreptitiously slid his gun out from beneath his seat as he pushed the button to open his window with the other.

"What are you doing here, Mr. Garrison? And you'd better have a pretty good explanation."

Sophie's stern voice oozed over his senses. The warmth from last night had been replaced by controlled but undisguised anger. She stood with both hands fisted on her hips. Yep, she was preparing for a fight, all right. He just didn't know if he was awake enough to provide one.

"Sophie? Is that you?" He slid his weapon beneath his belt,

snug against his back. Sophie stepped back as he swung the car door open and stepped outside.

Acting disoriented and sleepy, which really wasn't such a tough act since it was probably the first sleep he'd had in the past 48 hours, he staggered a step toward her. He made a show of glancing at her, then at her house and finally back to her.

"I could have sworn I was sitting outside Daisy Lee's house. I've been following her all week from one secret liaison to another. Boy, her husband's going to be mad that I made the wrong turn and missed where she disappeared to this time." He held his breath while he waited for her reaction.

Sophie blinked. His explanation wasn't what she'd expected and she wasn't quite sure how to respond. Was he serious? Did he really end up here by mistake? He did seem a bit disoriented and lethargic. Or was he just hoping she'd be stupid enough to swallow that explanation? Before she could make up her mind, he stepped into her personal space. He stood only inches from her. His body straightened to his full six-foot-two height, an energy and alertness quickly replacing any misconceptions she might have had about his lethargy. His head and shoulders loomed over her, blocking out the sun so there was nothing obstructing the cold, hard features glaring down at her.

"Why do you think I'm out here, darlin'?" His voice was so cold it could drip ice chips. "Couldn't be because I'm trying to protect one of the most stubborn women I've ever met, now could it?"

She drew in a breath and opened her mouth to protest but before she could utter a sound, he said, "What will it take to convince you that the things that have happened to you in the past two weeks are not a coincidence or the result of a bad dream? Every bone in my body wants to shake you silly until you understand this isn't a game. Lucky for you, shaking women is not one of my character traits. I have other methods for handling obstinate females." He leaned closer, his breath fanning her hair. "Want a lesson?"

Sophie's pulse raced and her own breath came in short, shallow gasps. She stumbled backward trying to break this hypnotic hold he seemed to have on her.

But he anticipated her and moved forward with her until only a feather could slip between them. His eyes locked with hers. His lips pulled back in a snarl. "What do I have to do to make you understand? You're in danger. Real let's-kill-your-dad, run-you-down-with-a-car and ransack-your-home danger. Get it?"

He waited a second for his words to sink in and then he stepped back. He ran a hand over the stubble on his face. He sighed and softened his tone. "Sophie, I like you. My sister likes you. We'd like to get to know you better. Neither one of us wants to attend your funeral."

He knew from the sudden pallor in her face that his words had hit home.

Anger seeped out of her body like a deflated balloon. She stared at him as confusion, fear and then something else—determination—flashed through her eyes. "Well, why are we standing out here? We have work to do. Come inside. Have some breakfast. The sooner we get started the better."

Cain stood in the kitchen doorway and took another look around the cottage. She must have worked all night. No one would ever know this place had been ransacked less than twenty-four hours ago. Yesterday, he'd helped her clean up the bulk of the mess but had still left her in a sea of clutter, pictures askew, broken frames. Not anymore.

He ended up in the living room and marveled at the warm and welcoming ambiance. The blue-and-green plaid sofa with its overstuffed pillows held center stage in the middle of the room and faced the fireplace. Two solid chairs, one green, one blue, rested on either side. Pictures had been rehung. Plants rearranged. Even the broken window, temporarily repaired with cardboard and duct tape, now sported a bright yellow patch of cloth to hide the repair.

"Would you like another cup?" Sophie stood next to him, the coffeepot in her hand. She smiled at how quickly he'd cleaned his plate but didn't comment.

"No, but thanks." He gestured to his empty plate. "When you said breakfast I thought maybe cereal or a bagel. Those eggs, bacon and home fries beat both my mom's and Holly's in a heartbeat."

A blush of pleasure tinged her face and he had to stifle the urge to reach out and trace his finger over the flush on her cheeks. She kept creeping under his skin—and he would keep pushing her out. Period.

"Breakfast is—was—is—Dad's favorite meal of the day." A cloud of sadness drifted over her face. Without another word, she turned and carried the coffeepot back to the counter.

Cain followed and placed his plate and cup in the sink.

"You're limping." Her gaze caught his and challenged him. "Worse today than yesterday."

He found it almost impossible to look away from the empathy and concern he saw in those beautiful green eyes. Not emerald, which could be sharp and cold. No, Sophie's eyes reminded him of a sea-green tropical ocean. Promising fun. Refreshment for the body and spirit. Yet, filled with hidden coves and secret treasures.

Snap out of it. What's the matter with you? Who cares what color her eyes are or what secrets they hide? Is that keeping it professional?

He drew a deep breath and stared down at his leg. "Between our skid across Main Street and a night cramped in the passenger well of my car, my leg's taken a beating. But it'll be fine."

"Can I get you something for the pain?"

"No, but thanks."

She chewed her lower lip and a worried expression flash across her face. Even with all her misgivings about him, she still had the sweetest heart, worrying about his leg, not knowing whether to push the issue of pain meds or let it drop. Sweet. Thoughtful. Caring.

Okay, enough. Cain closed his eyes. *Dear Lord, You've put this young woman in my path. Please let me guide and protect her. Chase away the human flaws and weaknesses that burden me. Don't let me ever forget what happened with Lucy, Lord. Let me never, ever forget.*

"Cain?"

He opened his eyes.

"Are you okay?" Small frown lines spread across her forehead and peaked right between her eyes.

"I'm sorry. I was just saying a quick morning prayer. I think we're going to need all the help we can get with this case." He clasped her elbow and steered her back toward the kitchen table. "Let's get to work."

When they were seated, Sophie asked, "So what's the first step? Are you going to do a title search on this house and prove it's mine?"

Her eagerness and anticipation brought a smile to his face. "No." Cain leaned back in his seat. "We'll let the sheriff save us the time and trouble on that one." She'd never make it as a detective. Ninety-five percent of his job was to hurry up and wait. Sometimes the tedium became downright boring. No, Sophie couldn't tolerate sitting still for any length of time, let alone being cooped in a car on a stakeout or behind a desk doing mountains of paperwork.

"I'm hoping the sheriff spends his time finding out that this house belongs to my mother before he turns his attention to locating my dad." Her voice grew soft, almost inaudible. "If he finds out Dad's missing—or worse, that his identity isn't what it should be—he just might think I don't have a right to be here. He wouldn't throw me out of my own home, would he?" She chewed on a fingernail and made an obvious effort not to squirm in her seat while she waited for Cain to reply.

"Don't worry about it, Sophie. If the sheriff asks you to leave, I'm sure it will be temporary until we get the answers to some of these questions. My parents have a five-bedroom home right off Main Street. The place stands empty most of the time, now that Holly and I have a place of our own. I'm certain they'd love to have you. You've met my dad. He's the town pharmacist. Mom owns the hair and nail salon right next door."

Move into town? Live with strangers?

Sophie's blood drained to her toes. Her legs trembled. She knew if she tried to stand she'd land flat on the ground in a hurry.

She didn't want to move into town. She certainly didn't want to move in with strangers. There was a world of difference between being friendly when you sold a piece of art to a person and actually sharing the same roof. She knew her social skills were good. She could discuss current events and carry on lively conversations with the best of them. But making friends—sharing personal thoughts and feelings—letting people get close—she'd never had the opportunity to do that before and the thought terrified her.

"Do you think that will happen?" Sophie's voice was a mere whisper. "Do you think the sheriff will throw me out of my home?"

Her eyes shone with terror. Her paleness made Cain wonder if she was about to be sick.

He reached across the table and clasped her hand. "It'll be okay, Sophie. No matter what happens, I promise it will be okay."

Sophie nodded. She cleared her throat, seemed to gather her resolve again and asked, "So we're letting the sheriff do the research on the title. What's our next move?"

Our next move, indeed. Cain didn't have one.

The Charlottesville police department had already done a thorough investigation into Anthony Clarkston and the road was a dead end. The man didn't exist. His identification papers were as phony as Sophie's. Cain was a good investigator. But he had no idea how to locate a man who was smart enough not to leave a paper trail. He hesitated to make the next statement but knew he must.

"We start searching each state morgue for unidentified male bodies."

She paled more, if that were possible, and simply nodded. "Good. I need to know—either way. Not knowing is torture. Can I help? I can make telephone calls or look things up on the internet or send emails. Whatever clerical stuff you need, I'm your gal."

Sophie Joy Clarkston climbed another rung on his admiration ladder.

"Have you looked through all your belongings?" Cain asked. "There must be something I can follow up on."

Sophie's eyes widened and she flapped her hands in excitement. "I almost forgot. Wait here."

She dashed from the room and returned almost before he noticed she'd left. "Look." She shook a photograph in front of his face. "I found this tucked away in my mother's Bible when I was cleaning up last night."

He took the faded, badly wrinkled photo from her hand and stared down at the aged image. The picture had been taken at a distance so the women's facial features weren't distinct. He studied the photo and could instantly see they were probably in their late teens. They stood, grinning ear to ear, in their bathing suits, their arms strewn across each other's shoulders.

He glanced up. "Okay, I'll bite. What's so exciting about this picture?"

"Don't you see?" Sophie grabbed a chair and scooted up beside him. She tapped the picture. "That's my mother. I recognize her from a photo my dad always carried in his wallet."

Cain's eyes followed the direction her finger pointed. He was immediately drawn to the woman standing in the middle of the photo. She was beautiful. The same long ebony hair. The same physical build. The same warm, friendly smile. And even though it wasn't a good quality picture he instinctively knew that those large, expressive eyes were sea-foam green.

"She's beautiful," Cain said.

"Duh, of course she is, silly." Sophie playfully elbowed him in the ribs. "But that's not why I wanted you to see this. She pointed her index finger to the background. "Look, that's this house. See. Recognize the front porch?"

Sophie sat back and grinned at him, apparently very pleased with herself.

"Don't you see? This picture proves this house belongs to my family. Besides, there are other people in the picture. Maybe they still live around here and can tell us something more about my mother."

Cain knew this photograph would not substantiate her claim to this property but preferred not to disappoint her. The sheriff would do that soon enough. Instead, he asked Sophie if she had a magnifying glass. He'd been raised in Promise. Even though he hadn't been born when this picture was taken, he knew almost everyone still in town. Maybe he'd be able to study the facial features and connect it with someone at church or someone he'd seen coming into Holly's Diner.

Sophie scampered into the living room and slid her hand down the flat side of a desk. Within seconds a hidden drawer popped out from the bottom.

Cain jumped up, quickly crossed the room and peered inside. He saw a magnifying lens and a stamp collection album inside. "I don't understand." Cain continued to stare at the drawer.

Sophie tilted her head to the side, a quizzical expression on her face. "Dad collected stamps. Is that important?"

"Maybe. I don't know. But that's immaterial at the moment."

Cain squatted down, mindful of the sharp jab of pain in his leg but doing his best to ignore it. He pushed the drawer back into place. The etchings on the wood hid the drawer and made it appear like nothing more than decorative embellishment.

"I've never seen anything quite like this. I would never have known a drawer was here." He admiringly ran his hand along the wood.

Sophie's shoulders puffed up with pride. "Dad made this desk. He put a hidden compartment in every single piece of wood he carved. It was like his signature. He developed quite a reputation on the craft circuit for that skill."

Every piece he carved. Cain straightened and took a second look around the cottage. Maybe that's why someone had broken into the house. Maybe they knew about the secret compartments. Obviously the thief had been searching for something. What if he hadn't found it? What if it was still hidden in one of the many pieces of hand-carved wood in the home? Cain felt his first inkling of hope since Sophie had walked into his office. At least now they had a place to start. A bread crumb to follow.

"Have you checked all the hiding places?" Cain couldn't curb his enthusiasm.

Sophie's eyes widened and then she grinned. "I will now."

Slowly, piece by piece, Sophie opened the hidden compartments on each carved piece within the home. Cain watched in fascination as picture frames slid apart, sofa legs sprang drawers and boxes revealed false bottoms. The carvings were all pieces of art. The hidden additions to the etchings were simply amazing. Unfortunately, nothing sinister or helpful showed up in any of the pieces.

Cain snapped his fingers. "What about the jewelry box?"

"Jewelry box? I don't own a jewelry box."

"The box. The one we found on the floor. The one you said was a gift from your dad." Cain's voice rose with excitement. He gently clasped her arms. "If your dad tried to hide a secret or a message for you, wouldn't he put it in that box?"

Sophie's eyes lit up. She nodded and hurried into her bedroom. When she returned, the way she cradled the object against her body and stroked the intricate carvings on the lid revealed her emotional attachment to this particular piece. She gently placed it on the kitchen table.

"It's not a jewelry box," she said. "It's a treasure chest." Her smile lit up her face. "Dad made it for me when I was a toddler."

He studied the carvings. It was a tiny replica of this house with toys scattered around the yard. Dolls. A ball. Even a tire swing. "It's beautiful, Sophie."

"I used to keep all sorts of things in here. Different shaped rocks. Especially smooth, shiny ones. Once I even kept a live frog until my dad found out and made me let it go." She threw her head back with laughter. "You should have seen his face when the frog jumped out. He chased it all over the cabin before he caught and released it." Suddenly, she sobered. "I miss him so much."

Cain paused, allowing her a moment with her memories before he said, "Show me. Where's the hidden compartment on this chest?" He held his breath in anticipation. Could it really be this easy? All the answers hidden right here in a child's treasure chest?

Sophie smiled. Slowly, she traced a finger along the top of the box, pushed down on the tire swing and a drawer ejected from the lid like a knife from a switchblade. Inside on a velvet-lining rested a cameo.

"I guess it's a jewelry box after all," Sophie said. "That cameo belonged to my mother. I've had it since I was a baby. Almost forgot it was there." She withdrew the locket, holding it in her hand and running her thumb along its surface.

Cain picked up the box. Surprised by its weight, he turned it upside down. Ran his hand inside the hidden drawer. Nothing. No clues. No secret notes or letters. Nothing.

He tried to hide his disappointment. He'd been certain if Sophie's dad had wanted to hide something that would lend a clue to his disappearance, it would have been in the box he knew his daughter cherished.

Cain didn't know what surprised him more, realizing his gut instincts weren't as sharp as they had been when he was on the force, or the surge of anger he felt toward Sophie's dad for leaving her in a world of unanswered questions and hurt.

"Is there anything else?" He asked through gritted teeth. "Anywhere we haven't already looked?"

Sophie gently placed her mother's locket back in the chest and pushed in the compartment lid. "Sorry, Cain. I've shown you everything."

Cain's heart clenched when he looked into her eyes and saw the deep sadness residing there. He wanted to help her. He wanted to see her eyes sparkle with laughter, not cloud with tears. But how? *Please, Lord, where do I go from here?*

"Think, Sophie. If your dad wanted to hide something that he *didn't* want you or anyone else to see, where would he put it?"

Sophie absently tapped her foot. Her eyes lit up and she grinned. "His tool box. No one, not even me, was ever allowed near his tools. I brought them with me when I came to Promise. The box is in the shed."

They both hurried across the porch and out to the shed in the backyard. The wooden box, large and cumbersome, took a bit of effort to lift to the table. Cain was amazed that petite, fragile Sophie had been able to do it previously. But then again, Cain was learning quickly that Sophie's tiny size might give her the appearance of fragility but nothing could be further from the truth. She had a backbone made of steel.

Sophie ran her hand across the lid. She hesitated before opening the secret panel, almost as if she wouldn't be able to face the disappointment if it was empty. She popped the lid, looked inside and grinned. But then her expression twisted with pain and confusion.

Cain came around the side of the box, eased Sophie away and looked inside. There were a dozen packets bound with rubber bands. Maybe two dozen. A picture of Sophie's father stared back from each packet. Cain unwrapped the top one and spread the contents on the table. Driver's license. Social security card. ATM card. A couple of credit cards. All in the name of Arthur Green. But the picture IDs beared the likeness of Sophie's father.

Then he opened a second packet bearing the missing man's likeness. Driver's license. Social security card. ATM card. All in the name of Jonathan Burke.

Third packet. Albert Covington.

Fourth packet. Anthony Trafficante.

Cain could barely stand the look of embarrassment and pain in Sophie's eyes.

"I don't understand." Her words were a mere whisper. She studied the identifying information. "It looks like my dad had a packet for each state on our craft circuit. Everyone on the circuit called him Woody, sort of a nickname because of his craft. I'd have had no way of knowing he had identification in different names." As the impact of this information hit her, she dropped the packet she was holding into the box. Her eyes welled with tears. "Excuse me." She turned and hurried into the house.

Cain gave her a few minutes and then followed her. He rapped lightly and leaned against the doorjamb. "Are you okay?"

Sophie paced back and forth. In her left hand she held a small wad of clay. He watched as she squeezed and turned and squeezed the material in a punishing grasp. She offered a tremulous smile and waved her right hand in the air. "Sure. Why wouldn't I be? My dad didn't have just one fake identity. He had a dozen of them. But, hey, if you're going to tell one lie, why not a dozen—or a hundred—or a million more?" Her cheeks flamed.

Cain hurried to her side. "Sophie." She continued to pace. When she swooped past him a second time he grasped her arm. "Stop."

She looked at him, her eyes haunted, lost.

"I can't imagine how hard this must be," Cain said. "To be forced to question everything you thought you knew about your dad and have him missing on top of it all."

She hitched a breath.

"But you're not alone. I'm going to help you. Holly will help you. Even the sheriff will help us run down some leads.

So hang tough. You've been doing great and I am proud of you."

Her eyes clouded with hesitation. He sensed her body tense as though steeling her mind for his answer and then she asked, "Do you think my dad is dead?"

He took a step back and raked his fingers through his hair. He knew she'd been lied to so many times that she needed to start hearing the truth. No matter how much he didn't want to be the one to tell her.

"Probably."

Her eyes widened but she said nothing.

"Look, all the facts lean that way. He leaves you enough money to take care of your needs for quite some time. Leaves you a note stating someone is trying to kill him. Then he disappears without a trace." He held his hands at his side when everything in him wanted to wrap her in his arms and comfort her. "You tell me, Sophie. Who has fake IDs? Teenagers, maybe. Trying to pretend they're older than they are to obtain alcohol." He took a step closer as though his nearness could soften the blow. "Who else, Sophie? People on the run? Hiding. Slipping quietly from one town to the next, never setting down roots in one spot."

Sophie paled. Her lower lip trembled but she kept control and stood tall, not speaking, just staring at him with those wide sea-green eyes, until he felt like dirt for hurting her.

"You told me that the two of you had been inseparable since your mother's death," he continued. "Don't you think that if your dad was lucky enough to escape whoever was trying to kill him, he would have contacted you by now—some way—somehow?"

He studied her quietly for a moment, letting his words sink in.

"Sophie, I promise I will always tell you the truth, even if I know the truth will hurt. People have lied to you long enough." He paused for just a moment. "I'm sorry. I really am. But the evidence leads me to believe your dad is dead."

She stood quietly for a few moments and then nodded. "Thank you, Cain, for being honest. The truth means everything to me right now." She transferred the clay to her right hand and continued kneading. Cain surmised it was something she did to calm her nerves when she was under stress.

"I need to know what happened to my father. I need to find my dad, dead or alive. I won't be able to put any of this behind me until I find out what happened to him and what this is all about." She walked over to the kitchen counter, hesitated for a few moments, her head bent, her shoulders stooped. Then pulling on that inner resolve he so admired, she squared her shoulders, poured two mugs of hot coffee and turned to face him. "We have work to do. Let's get at it."

Cain sat down at the table and Sophie placed a mug at his elbow. He nodded, offered a quick thanks and took a sip. Placing the mug back down, he picked up the photo they'd discarded when they'd run out to the shed and lifted the magnifying lens.

"I'm not giving up," he said, trying to keep his voice light and encouraging. "You don't know it yet but you've hired the best detective in Virginia."

Sophie tried unsuccessfully to return his smile.

Cain pulled the photograph in for a closer look. He held the magnifying glass above the image of the young girl standing on the left of Sophie's mother. She was a cute girl. About sixteen, seventeen maybe. He slowly studied her facial features. Try as he might, he couldn't get a clear picture in his mind of what the girl would look like today. Granted, knowing that Sophie was twenty-two meant this picture was anywhere from twenty-five to thirty or more years old. These three women would be in their late fifties, maybe early sixties. So he didn't have to imagine snow-white hair, wrinkles and stooped shoulders. They still should resemble their teen pictures enough for recognition. Cain ran the lens over the figure on the left again. Nope. He couldn't ever remember seeing this person in Promise.

"Anything?" Sophie leaned against his arm, trying to stare into the magnifying lens with him. He could feel the heat of her body. He breathed in the lilac scent on her skin. An unwanted awareness raced through his bloodstream. It took all his control to subtly move back in his chair, breaking their contact and not letting her know how her nearness had affected him.

"Nothing yet. Sorry." Again, Cain picked up the glass. But when he saw Sophie getting ready to lean in again to look at the picture, he knew he had to distract her. "Do you have any cookies?"

"Cookies?" Sophie sat back, an astonished look on her face.

"Yeah. Cookies. Toast. I like crunchy food with my coffee."

Sophie laughed. The sweet, tinkling sound filled the cabin and did nothing to deter his acute awareness of her. "Okay, cookies it is. But I get to deduct the cost of food from your bill," she teased as she scampered into the kitchen.

Cain grabbed the picture for a quick look before she returned. He held the lens over the third woman in the photo and leaned in for a closer look. *Nope. Don't know this one, either.* Cynicism rose up in him. Of course it wouldn't be this easy. When was life ever easy? Then he stamped down those unproductive thoughts and tried to brainstorm another solution to the problem.

"Anything?" Sophie mumbled, busily munching away on a chocolate chip cookie and offering him one from a small plate in her hand.

He waved the cookies away. The distraction had served its purpose. "No. But I've got an idea. Grab your things and come with me."

SEVEN

A sound at the door of Cain's office drew Sophie's attention and she looked up from the yearbook she'd been studying.

"Anything?" Cain came through the door with at least a dozen more books in his arms, which he dumped unceremoniously on the edge of the desk.

"No. Not yet." She rubbed her eyes with the back of her hands and tried to muffle her sigh. She'd been sitting for hours trying to match the faces of the girls in the photo she'd found in her mother's Bible with the yearbook pictures.

"Where are you getting all these books?" she asked.

"Mrs. Neville, the town librarian. If you're looking for any book on any subject, she won't stop until she tracks it down."

"Wouldn't it have been easier to look through these books at the library instead of dragging all of them over here?"

"Absolutely." Cain leaned back in one of the leather chairs and made a show of opening a yearbook. "But Mrs. Neville would have been staring over our shoulders, peppering us with questions and then spreading stories all over town. I don't think it's a good idea to ruin the element of surprise just in case we do locate the girls."

"So what did you do to get her to let you bring all these

books over here? And shouldn't the books be at the high school instead of the library?"

"Mr. Fenton runs the high school. He's a clean freak. Organizer from hell. Honestly, he even calls biweekly locker inspections and bans the kids from using their lockers if they're cluttered. These books are over twenty years old. He would have thrown them out. Mrs. Neville prides herself on saving high school history by keeping the yearbooks in the library storage room."

"And she gave them to you because…?"

"I told you. I have a unique way of dealing with obstinate women. Want a lesson?"

Sophie laughed. "No, thanks. I'll pass." She turned her attention back to the book in front of her, looked through the last two pages and slammed it closed. "Nothing."

"Don't give up. All three girls lived in Promise at one time or another. At least one of them must have graduated from the local high school. We just have to match our photo to the girl's yearbook photo and we'll have a name."

"I'm not giving up." Sophie rubbed her eyes again. "But this is the third book I've gone through and I'm getting worried. What if I'm missing something?"

"You're not missing anything. I've watched you stare at each and every photo so hard you can probably tell me if they have a zit on their nose." He slid another book across the desk and then opened one of his own. They'd been scouring the pages in front of them for only a few minutes when a loud growl from Sophie's stomach broke the silence.

Cain laughed and then glanced at his watch. "Five o'clock. We've worked straight through lunch. What do you say we take a break and grab some dinner? I have an inside source who assures me tonight is homemade pot roast at Holly's diner."

Sophie grinned. "And I was beginning to think you were

a machine and didn't need common sustenance like other mere humans." Careful to bookmark her place, she stood and followed him from the office.

Sophie didn't know what pleased her more—the exuberant welcome from Holly when they entered the diner or the delectable aroma of cooked beef and onions wafting through the room. Her heart responded to the first, her stomach painfully growled at the second.

"Do you want to sit in a booth or at the counter?" Cain asked.

"Sit at the counter, Sophie, so we can talk." Holly, her T-shirt and jeans covered by a large white apron, swiped a cloth across the counter and had already dropped two napkin-wrapped bundles of silverware in the appropriate spots.

Sophie perched on the edge of the red-and-chrome bar stool and looked around. Most of the diners were deep in conversation with each other or busily eating their food. A couple here and there threw a less than friendly glance her way but Sophie chose to ignore them. She hadn't broken her grandfather's heart. She hadn't even had the opportunity to meet him.

"So, what's up? Any hot leads on the break-in?" Holly planted her elbows on the counter, her hands supporting her face, and grinned.

"Nope. Nothing yet." Caught up in Holly's enthusiasm, Sophie added, "But we found a picture I think is going to help. It's of my mother and two teenage girls in front of the Weatherly cottage. We think they might still be here in Promise."

"Cool. I told you my brother was a top-notch investigator. You're in good hands with him." Holly held out her hand to Cain. "You owe me five bucks for the testimonial. Pay up."

Cain playfully slapped her palm. "I'll pay up when I see two large plates of pot roast sitting in front of us."

Holly's laughter lingered after she moved away to get the food.

"I hope you don't mind me ordering for you," Cain said. "All the food served here is good, affordable and decently portioned—but the pot roast is something special."

"You only say that because you're the chef." Holly, back in a flash, placed two steaming plates in front of them.

Sophie stared at Cain and struggled to keep her surprise in check. "You cooked this?"

"I did."

"That's his sole contribution to being my partner. Every Tuesday he provides the pot roast special," Holly said.

"My only contribution?" Cain asked, feigning indignation. "Seems to me that most of the red, black and white decor in this place came from a little bit of green in my bank account."

Holly laughed. "Yeah, well, that, too."

"The two of you own this diner?" Sophie asked.

"Yep," Cain replied. "I step in occasionally and help run the place but mostly I'm a silent partner—except for pot roast Tuesdays."

"I don't know about the silent part," Holly teased. "But it's true. Mostly, he lets me run things. And I let him run the P.I. business unless he has an odd job that needs a female touch. Our individual talents fill in the gaps for each other's weaknesses. It makes the arrangement work."

Sophie's stomach growled again.

Cain and Holly laughed.

"Let me let you two eat. I'll be back again in a couple of minutes to see if there's anything else you need."

Sophie stared at her plate and felt like Pavlov's dog. The sight of the thick hunks of meat, red potatoes, hunks of carrots and celery combined with the rich, beefy aroma actually made her salivate. Unable to wait another second she took a bite and knew instantly that if she lived to be one hundred she'd never be able to cook as good as this.

She took a second bite. A third. And before she knew it, she had drowned out all the sights and sounds around her and done some serious eating. She was sopping the last remnants of gravy with her roll when she heard Cain chuckling beside her.

"I guess I don't have to ask if you liked it. You attacked that plate like a starving orphan. Any second now, I expect to hear you ask for more."

A rush of heat flowed through Sophie's cheeks and down her neck. To hide her embarrassment, she smiled up at him and attempted to change the subject. "An ex-cop. A private investigator. A chef. You're a complicated man, aren't you, Cain? A man of many surprises."

Raw emotion flashed across Cain's face. He leaned closer. His voice low. His breath fanning across her cheeks. "You have no idea, Miss Clarkston, just how complicated this all feels to me right now."

Her cheeks flamed. Somehow the conversation had abruptly steered from food to, what? Attraction? More? Sophie drew in a deep breath. She dared to look at him and saw her answer in the darkened eyes staring back.

Before either one of them could move—or even breathe—the sound of a siren sliced through the air. Red-and-blue strobe lights danced through the diner windows and most of the occupants strained to see what was going on outside.

Holly raced around the counter and cupped her eyes against the glass on the opposite wall. "It's the Falcon kid again." She shook her head from side to side. "Mom's going to be so disappointed."

Sophie arched an eyebrow in a silent question.

"Mom runs a craft workshop Sunday afternoons at the church for troubled teens," Cain explained. "She hopes finding constructive things to do with their time and talents will keep some of the borderline delinquents from crossing the line into the criminal justice system. Jimmy Falcon is one of her kids."

"The boy's bad news," Holly said. "He's got major anger issues. Painting a picture or working on leather isn't going to help with that."

"C'mon, Holly, give the guy a break. We both know why he has that temper. We might be just as angry if our mom ran off and our dad was a drunk."

Holly shrugged. "Still don't think arts and crafts is the way to tame that wild beast. He needs a good swift kick in his…"

"Holly!" Cain laughed. "Be careful. Any swearing and you'll find yourself in Mom's remedial class yourself."

"Derriere. I was going to say derriere."

"Sure you were." Cain stood and threw some bills on the counter.

"Since when do you pay for your dinner?" Holly scooped up the bills before he could change his mind.

Cain ignored the jibe, nodded a good-bye and cupped Sophie's elbow. "Let's go. We still have dozens of smiling yearbook pictures waiting for us."

As they stepped out of the diner, Sophie's eyes met and held with a young male teenager leaning over the trunk of the sheriff's car. The sheriff handcuffed his hands behind his back. Others might have seen rebellion and anger reflected in those eyes. Sophie recognized other feelings…feelings she'd experienced herself—pain—loneliness—fear.

"What do you think he did?" Sophie asked Cain as they crossed the street together.

Cain glanced at the law enforcement cars and the multiple teenagers gathered. "Drag racing would be my bet. It's been a real problem in our town lately. Some cities have gangs. We have punks with speed issues. We've had two deaths in the past year and one kid is in the hospital as we speak. But do they stop?"

"Your mom works with these kids?"

"She tries. She's had a few success stories. I guess that's what keeps her going." Cain looked over his shoulder at the dark-haired youth being shepherded into the backseat of the sheriff's cruiser. "That's Jimmy Falcon all right. She had high hopes for him. Too bad."

Once back at the office, they settled into the quiet routine of searching the yearbooks, but Sophie found it difficult to concentrate. She kept thinking of the pain she had seen in the boy's eyes.

"Penny for your thoughts," Cain said.

His voice pulled her out of her reverie. "Sorry. I was just thinking about your mom and her arts and crafts classes. Do you know if she ever introduced working with clay to the teens?"

Cain leaned back and threw an arm over the back of his chair. "I don't know. Why?"

Sophie shrugged. "No reason, really." She squirmed under his silent scrutiny. "It's just that I've found clay is a very soothing medium. There's nothing quite like pounding it and shaping it from its raw form into something unique and beautiful."

"Wouldn't that be a little complicated for these kids?"

"Not at all. They can start out with the clay squares you get in arts and crafts stores. There are lots of how-to books available. Even a beginner can make beads for jewelry or little figurines." Her eyes lit up as she spoke. "You can develop quite a sense of accomplishment when you squeeze and mold a lump of clay and make it come alive. I believe it could really help a kid forget his anger or loneliness, if only for a little while."

"Is that why I see you knead modelling clay every now and then? Working off steam?"

Her eyes shot to his and she felt vulnerable, like he'd seen a glimpse of her that she'd never shared with anyone before. "Something like that," she said. "Pounding clay beats pounding heads. It's a great stress reliever."

"I imagine moving as often as you did was quite stressful. Never gave you the sense of having roots. Never let you form lasting friendships."

"It wasn't that bad. At least my dad isn't the town drunk. And we did make friends—on the craft circuit. We'd see the same people every year."

Cain stared at her long and hard as though he could see right through her. Without a word, she lowered her head and returned to the task at hand.

Two books later, when she'd decided this was a fool's mission and was ready to throw in the towel, a familiar face smiled up at her from the page. She blinked, stared harder and blinked again.

A rush of excitement danced along her nerve endings. She picked up the photo in her left hand and a magnifying lens in her right. Comparing the face in the photograph with the picture in the yearbook, she grinned.

"Cain. We've found her."

He circled the table and peered over her shoulder. He looked through the large magnifying lens at the image of a smiling teenager. A quick glance at the photo in Sophie's left hand confirmed they'd found their match.

Cain picked up the book for a closer look. "Andrea Patterson."

"Do you know her?"

"No. But it shouldn't be too hard to track her down. A couple of minutes on the computer and we should have what we need."

"Great." Sophie bounced up from her chair. "Let's do it."

Cain laughed, placed a hand on her shoulder and eased her back into her chair. "Whoa, speed racer. We're not doing anything right now."

She could barely conceal her disappointment.

He glanced at his watch. "Sorry, Sophie, but it's almost eight o'clock. The library closes at nine and I have to return these books, or Mrs. Neville will hunt me down and the punishment won't be pretty. Besides, it's time to get you home. Tomorrow is another day."

Sophie grimaced. *Tomorrow is another day.* So many times her father had said those exact words when she'd been antsy and excited about an upcoming craft show or a special treat. She missed him so much.

"You're right." She stood slowly and stacked the discarded yearbooks. "Let me help you take these back to the library. Who knows? Maybe I'll get to see you and your secret weapon in action."

The trip home passed in a companionable silence, each of them lost in their own thoughts. When they pulled up in front of Sophie's cottage, a flush of pleasure raced through her. This was home. The only home she'd ever known, and it surprised her how good it felt to be able to stay for more than a fleeting visit.

Cain exited and started checking the outside perimeter of the house before Sophie had even stepped from the car. *Once a cop, always a cop...and a private investigator...and a chef...and a really kind, decent man.* She couldn't hide the smile pulling at the corners of her mouth.

"Safe and sound?" she asked as Cain circled around from the back.

"So far, so good." He held out his hand for her key.

Once inside, Cain quickly moved from room to room,

checking windows, closets. He even peered behind the shower curtain in her bathroom.

Sophie lounged against a door jamb to the living room. "If P.I. doesn't work out for you, I'd be happy to give you a recommendation as security consultant."

Cain grinned. "Who said P.I. wasn't working?"

Sophie raised her hands defensively. "Point taken."
He hesitated by the front door and she raised an eyebrow in question.

"I'm not comfortable leaving you alone out here. I really wish you'd move to town—at least for a few days."

"Cain, you locked every window yourself. You checked every inch of the house that was big enough to hide a mouse. You paced the outside perimeter—twice. Now, go home. I am perfectly safe. I have 911 and your number on speed dial and pepper spray in my pocket."

She placed her hands against his chest and pushed lightly. The rock-solid hardness beneath her palms sent an unexpected thrill through her fingertips and she snatched back her hands as though she'd been burned. To hide her embarrassment, she opened the door and held it wide.

"Go. Now."

He stared at her with that dark intensity that made her feel he could read her emotions as easily as people read books.

"Don't go outside for anything." He stepped into the door threshold. "And don't open your door for anyone."

"Yes, sir." She gave him a mock salute. When he hit the bottom step of her porch she called, "Cain."

Instantly he stopped and turned.

"If I find you sleeping in your car again, you're fired."

He grinned. "Yes, ma'am. Now get inside."

She locked the dead bolt and then peered through the side window until Cain's car taillights were nothing more than a tiny red glow. Only when they'd disappeared completely did she allow her gaze to travel high and low over the surrounding trees and shrubs.

Nothing.

No sounds.

No unusual shadows.

She was safe.

So why couldn't she shake this strong sensation that the woods had eyes?

EIGHT

Sophie hoped Cain would blame the bright morning sun for the red tinge in her cheeks and not realize this blush occurred each time she looked at him.

"I could have driven my own car and met you at your office." She enjoyed the freedom of studying his profile unnoticed as he drove—his sharp cheekbones, straight nose and strong chin, the shadow of a beard although he'd obviously shaved this morning. Cain looked so much like a young Johnny Depp. The resemblance was amazing—and to think she'd found him in the tiny town of Promise, Virginia. Who knew?

"Andrea Patterson lives out this way," Cain said. "We're both going to the same place, right? Why waste time or gas?"

"According to you, nobody in their right mind lives out this way except me."

Cain chuckled. "Point taken."

When he turned his head and smiled, her stomach flip-flopped. She wondered if he had this effect on the entire female population or if the powerful draw she felt for him was the beginning of something special. Sophie wasn't that naive. She knew he was fighting his attraction to her as well.

What was it? She'd seen good-looking men before, even

dated a couple of them, but she'd never experienced such conflicting emotions. She had to keep reminding herself that she had hired him to find her father. Period. It was foolish to allow her emotions to enter the picture. Yet, his personality drew her to him. As well as his strength, intelligence, compassion. She couldn't deny the entire package had the makings for some pretty strong chemistry.

Chemistry? Insanity, maybe. After all, she'd only known the man for three days. Although she had to admit they'd been terrifying, adventurous, exciting days. She gave herself a mental shake. Her nomadic and reclusive life had made it rare to be exposed to a man like Cain, that was all. She needed to acknowledge that the attraction was normal—like appreciating the beauty of a sunset or a finished sculpture—and then get her head out of the clouds.

"I can't believe you located her address this quickly," Sophie said, attempting to bring her mind back to business, not biceps.

"Ahh, the beauty of modern technology." Cain grinned again. "It took a little doing since she's married now and changed her name. But give me access to the internet and a telephone and no one can hide from me."

Sophie hitched a breath. She knew from the darkening of his skin and the scowl on his face that he regretted the words as soon as they'd slipped from his lips.

"Sorry, Sophie." He glanced her way and then back to the road.

"No problem." Sophie tried to keep her voice light. "I hired you for those exact skills. I'm counting on you locating my dad, remember?"

He nodded but his demeanor suggested he continued to regret his thoughtlessness.

"So," Sophie began, trying to change the subject and lighten the mood, "What did you say to her? Is she expecting us? Did she remember the picture? Did she remember my mother?"

"Whoa, Sophie. Time out." Cain laughed. "I know you're excited but you have to calm down."

"I'm calm." She tapped her foot in the passenger well. "Tell me. What did she say?"

"She didn't say anything." Cain smiled indulgently. "I thought the conversation should be done in person. Sometimes body language is as important during an interview as the actual words a person speaks."

Sophie nodded.

"I told her I was a private investigator and would greatly appreciate her help on a case. She's as excited and curious as you are. Most people in Promise don't get a telephone call like that every day. She'll be burning up the phone lines the second we leave to share her fifteen minutes of fame."

Cain had no sooner spoken those words than they saw a thin woman in her mid-fifties appear on the porch as they pulled up to the house. She patted her hair and straightened her skirt. Then she held her fingers over her eyes to block the sun as they exited the car.

"You must be Mr. Garrison," she called, excitement evident in her voice. "You're right on time. Come have a seat. I have coffee, tea, cookies." She ushered them onto the porch and Sophie bit her lip to hide her grin at how accurate Cain had been about the woman without ever having met her.

"This is my associate, Ms. Clarkston," Cain said as the three of them sat down. He accepted a cup of coffee and took a cookie from the offered plate. "We won't take much of your time, Mrs. Carter."

"Oh, my, that's quite all right, young man." Mrs. Carter offered the cookie plate to Sophie and then sat down opposite them. She perched on the edge of her seat, barely able to contain her curiosity. "I must admit I was surprised when I got your telephone call. I can't imagine what important case you're working on that I can help with."

Sophie ducked her head and bit her lip harder. Somehow she didn't think Cain had painted the picture with the same mystique and excitement that this woman's own mind had conjured up. She just hoped that the woman's memory was as active and intact as her imagination.

Cain sipped his coffee, put down the cup and then withdrew a photo from his jacket pocket. "Do you recognize this picture?"

The woman adjusted her glasses and took a long look at the picture.

"Of course I do. Wherever did you get this?"

Cain withheld the answer and asked, "Can you tell me about it? When was it taken? Or where?" He tapped the edges of the photo. "Do you remember the names of the other people in the picture with you?"

Mrs. Carter's face twisted in concentration as she studied the photograph and then handed it back. "That picture was taken years ago out at the old Weatherly place. That's me." She pointed to a figure in the photo. "This is Elizabeth and this is Karen." She sent Cain a questioning glance. "Why? What are you doing with this picture?"

"It belonged to my mother," Sophie blurted. "Elizabeth Weatherly. Do you remember her?"

Mrs. Carter turned her attention to Sophie. She squinted her eyes. "I'm sorry. I really didn't know your mother. I had just met her earlier that day. My goodness, it had to be more than twenty years ago. I don't see what it has to do with anything now."

"Mrs. Carter." Cain took back control of the interview. "Can you name the other woman in the photo with you?"

"Karen Anderson."

"Does she still live in town?"

"No. Karen moved away years ago." Mrs. Carter folded her hands on her lap and stared at Cain. "What's this all about, anyway?"

Cain gave her his most endearing smile. "I'm doing some research for the Weatherly family. We're focusing right now on Elizabeth and we're only interviewing those special, close friends from days gone by." He stopped talking and seemed to be letting his charming smile disarm any opposition the woman might have been having to his interrogation.

"Well, I don't know where you got your information about me being a close friend but it's wrong."

Cain blinked but otherwise showed no reaction to her words.

"Karen invited me to join her at the Weatherly place for a swim. I had just met Elizabeth. She seemed like a nice enough girl but it really was the only time I'd ever met her."

Another dead end.

"Really?" Cain crossed his ankle over his knee. "Didn't you go to school together?"

"Not really. We never had any classes together. That picture was taken at the end of the summer. When school started in the fall, Elizabeth had already left."

"Left?"

"Run off. Eloped. Depends on what town gossip you listen to." She glanced over at Sophie. "Sorry, honey. But you must know this story already, considering you're Elizabeth's daughter."

Cain leaned forward, drawing her attention. "Mrs. Carter, do you remember the name of the boy Elizabeth ran away with?"

Mrs. Carter rubbed her chin and stared into space. Finally she looked back at the two of them. "Sorry. Can't say I do."

She stared at Sophie and it was obvious from the expression on her face that she wondered why Sophie didn't already have the information. "Besides, it wasn't a boy. She ran off with a man. That's what caused such an uproar. Your grand-daddy called the sheriff. If I remember correctly, they had search parties scour the woods. Even put up roadblocks. But she had already disappeared."

Cain braced himself as he glanced over at Sophie. He didn't know how she'd bear up under another disappointment. But she surprised him. Other than the slight flush to her cheeks, she seemed composed, calm, accepting.

Cain stood. "Thanks, Mrs. Carter. I'm sorry we bothered you."

"Oh, it was no bother." The woman stood, smoothed her hair and smiled at them. "It isn't every day a bona fide private investigator comes calling."

Sophie thanked her and preceded Cain down the porch steps. They'd reached the car when Mrs. Carter called out.

"I'm sorry I couldn't help you."

"That's okay," Cain said. He waved at the woman as he opened his car door. Sophie had already slid into the passenger seat.

"If you still have questions, maybe you should ask the person who took the picture."

Cain froze half in and half out of the car. Why hadn't he thought of that? He plopped down on the seat and leaned his head out the window. "Do you remember who took the picture, Mrs. Carter?"

"Sure, I do. Martha Barker."

"Are you sure?" Cain couldn't keep the surprise from his voice. He felt Sophie's eyes fix on him.

"Of course I'm sure. She was a real shutterbug back then. You never saw Martha without a camera in her hands. She worked as a photographer for the school paper. I think she still lives in town. Maybe she'll remember something about Elizabeth."

"Thanks again, Mrs. Carter. You've been a big help."

Sophie squirmed in the seat beside him but he admired the fact that she refrained from questioning him until they'd backed out of the driveway and were headed back to town.

Cain drummed his fingers on the steering wheel. His mind raced in a thousand different directions.

"You know her, don't you, Cain?"

"Yes."

"Great. Maybe she'll know something. Does she still live here in town? Who is she?"

Cain glanced at Sophie and then returned his attention to the road. "The shutterbug is Martha Barker. She married straight out of high school. Her married name is Martha Garrison—my mother."

NINE

"Your mother?" Sophie asked.

"I don't know why I was so surprised. Truthfully, I should have thought of it sooner. My parents were born and raised in Promise. They know just about everybody." Cain grinned. "I bet your mom and mine had the same teachers. Promise is a small town, but back then it was even smaller."

Sophie picked up the photo and stared at the image. "Do you think your mom will remember my mother?" She couldn't hide the wistfulness in her voice. "I've never met anyone other than my father who could tell me anything about her."

"Well, there's only one way to find out." Cain took the picture from her fingers and slid it into his shirt pocket. "Let's go ask her."

"Now?" She tucked her hair behind her ear and grimaced as she looked down at her T-shirt and jeans. A wave of panic washed over her. How should one dress when meeting a woman who could hold all the answers to the millions of questions in her heart? How well had Cain's mother known hers? Would she remember her? Would she be able to fill in the blanks, answer all of her questions about a woman who had mattered so much to her and yet whom she'd never met? And would Martha Garrison know anything about her father's real identity? Or hers?

"Hey," Cain gave her a playful tap on the arm. "Don't look so scared. My mom doesn't bite. I'll give her a call and ask her to meet us at the house." He lifted his cell phone.

Sophie reached out and grabbed his arm. "Wait!"

Cain held the phone in midair and stared at her.

"I…I want to meet your mother. I do," she said. "But I want to visit my mother first."

Cain lowered the phone and raised an eyebrow. "Your mother is buried in Promise? I don't understand. She isn't buried in the Weatherly family plot?"

Sophie smiled at his puzzled expression. "No. She's buried in Crossroads Cemetery under her married name of Clarkston. Dad thought it would be better that way. We'd come back to Promise twice a year and visit her grave. We were never here more than a week or so…but I still think of Promise as my home." She fought back the tears burning her eyes. "Or at least it used to be. In the days when I thought I was a Clarkston. Now I don't know who I am and I don't have anywhere to call home."

"Home is where your heart is, Sophie. And it sounds to me like Promise fits that bill." He gently rubbed her shoulder. "I'd be honored to go with you to visit your mother."

Sophie squatted down, placed the handpicked bouquet of flowers on the grave and ran her fingers across the name Elizabeth Ann Clarkston on the headstone.

"I'm here, Mom. I know it's not one of my usual visits and Dad's not with me this time but I'm here. I wish I could talk to you and tell you all the horrible things that have been happening and ask you for your advice."

She glanced up at Cain standing at the edge of the grave, turned back to the headstone and lowered her voice to a mere whisper. "I'm afraid, Mom. I'm so afraid. And the worst part of it all…" She glanced over her shoulder again and saw that Cain had walked a few feet away to give her privacy.

"Everything's one big lie. I'm not Sophie Clarkston. I don't have a clue who I really am." She stood and stared down at her mother's grave. "Did you know, Mom? Or did Dad lie to you, too?"

A breeze blew across the back of Sophie's neck and sent a shiver down her spine. Someone was watching her. Quickly, she swiveled her head and looked around. Cain stood about four graves away, his back to her, looking out at the horizon. To her left, some distance away, she saw an elderly woman holding a Bible at another grave. They seemed to be the only people on the grounds.

Sophie's eyes skimmed the rows of graves and trees for anything sinister. She *knew* someone was watching her. These eerie, uncomfortable sensations were not figments of her imagination. Whether she could see anyone or not, she knew she wasn't alone…that someone, somewhere was watching her every move.

"You okay?"

Sophie, startled by the unexpected sound of a voice, jumped and then laughed. "You scared me. You shouldn't be sneaking up on people, especially in cemeteries."

Cain laughed. "Point taken. Are you ready to go? I'm anxious to see if my mother can give us any information."

Sophie nodded. She glanced over her shoulder once more and then followed Cain to the car.

The view as they wound their way down the mountain was breathtaking. Promise, nestled in the valley beneath them, had grown and expanded in little bits at a time over the years. When she was a child, she used to think that Promise looked like a collection of miniature dollhouses in the palm of God's hand. In the days when she'd been certain there was a God.

Sophie sighed deeply. She knew God existed. How could

anyone take a look at this magnificent view of mountains and valley, blue sky and streams, and not feel the strong presence of a higher power? But like a spoiled child who didn't get her way, she was finding it difficult not to be angry at Him for leaving her on her own during the worst time of her life.

She sensed more than felt Cain tense beside her. She looked over at him and asked, "Everything okay?"

He eased his foot off the accelerator, his gaze bouncing back and forth from the rearview to the side mirror.

"Cain?"

"It's okay. I'm going to slow down and give this guy behind me a chance to pass."

"Pass? On a twisting two-lane highway? You think that's smart? Can't he wait until we get to the bottom to pass?"

Before Cain could reply, the car behind them tapped their bumper.

Sophie squealed and reached her hand out to steady herself against the dashboard. The drop off the side of the mountain loomed in her peripheral vision.

Cain muttered something unintelligible under his breath, pulled the car over as far as he dared and hung his arm out the window to wave the other car around him.

Instead, the car butted them again…harder this time.

Cain wrenched the wheel and moved his car away from the guardrail and into the middle of the road.

As they sped up and twisted around a bend, Sophie offered a silent prayer that no one was coming in the opposite direction. And offered a second prayer that if He never listened to any of her other prayers He would listen to this one.

Without warning, the car behind pulled alongside them, inching them toward the guardrail. It was all happening so quickly Sophie could barely get her bearings. She tried to see who sat behind the wheel of the other vehicle but the tinted windows prevented her from seeing inside. She took a good hard look and her stomach twisted in knots. It was a black, four-door sedan, just like the car that had tried to run her down.

The sound of screeching metal wrenched the air as Sophie's side of the car scraped against the guardrail.

Cain twisted the steering wheel, forcing the driver's side to slam against their attacker.

Again they were forced back against the guardrail.

Suddenly, a small blue sports car appeared behind the black sedan. Sophie couldn't believe her eyes when the sports car slammed into the black sedan, hurling it forward. The dull, deep metallic thud of the two cars impacting echoed through the air.

Immediately, the black sedan sped up and pulled in front of Sophie and Cain. The blue car stayed parallel to Cain's.

Cain's jaw clenched and his knuckles whitened as he hit the brakes. Their car skidded and swerved. The squeal of brakes and the smell of burning rubber filled the air.

The blue car sped up, passed theirs and raced the black sedan neck and neck down the winding road until both cars disappeared around a curve.

By this time Cain had skidded to a halt, leaving half their tires' tread along the highway.

Sophie's heart thundered inside her chest. What had just happened? She turned to look at Cain. Anger seemed to seep out of his every pore.

"It's over. We're all right," she assured him.

Cain slapped his hand against the steering wheel and stepped out of the car. Sophie quickly followed.

"Did you know those guys?"

"No," Cain replied. "But I'm going to." He pulled out his cell phone and punched in a number.

"Cain…it probably is a coincidence, but did you notice…?"

"That it was the same black sedan that tried to run you

down three days ago." His jaw looked etched from granite. His eyes glittered like glaciers. "Yeah, I noted that little fact."

"And the blue car?"

"An idiot teen who thought he'd lucked out and come upon some drag racers and decided to join the party? Who knows?"

Sophie sighed. Her limbs shook uncontrollably and she could barely stand. If that wasn't bad enough, now she was going to have to face Sheriff Dalton—again. Every time she thought she was having the worst day in history, the next day dawned worse than the one before. When was it all going to end?

Sophie sat on the guardrail and pulled cold water deep into her throat from the bottle the sheriff had handed her after she gave her statement. The icy liquid soothed her parched throat. She wiped her mouth with the back of her hand. "Thanks."

"No problem." The sheriff hooked his thumbs into his belt and rocked slightly back and forth. "Seems like you keep getting yourself into a heap of trouble, young lady."

"Me? I'm the victim, Sheriff, not the bad guy." She cupped her fingers over her eyes to shield them from the sun as she looked into his mirrored sunglasses. Sophie hated mirrored sunglasses. You could never see the person's eyes.

"So Cain tells me."

"Well, Cain tells me you have problems with teens drag racing in the streets."

"That we have, Ms. Clarkston. But even our dumbest teenagers wouldn't be stupid enough to play chicken on a mountain."

Sophie could feel the blood drain out of her face. "You don't think it was teenagers racing?"

"Do you?" The large hulking man intimidated her. He

must be scary as all get-out during a formal interrogation. She sure hoped she'd never have to find out.

"I don't know what to think, Sheriff. All I know is one car hit us. A second car hit them. And they raced away. That's about all the excitement I want to think about today."

He scribbled a note in the small pad he carried and put it back in his pocket. "The thing is I was on my way to your house anyway. Checked with the title company. The cottage is definitely registered to Elizabeth Weatherly. The problem, little lady, is that I haven't been able to find anything telling me you have a right to be living in that cottage. I haven't been able to locate a marriage license in the name of Elizabeth Weatherly Clarkston. I haven't been able to locate a birth certificate for a Miss Sophie Clarkston. And strangest of all, I haven't been able to locate your daddy. Now why do you think that is?"

Sophie clenched her hands together and tried not to hyperventilate. Instead of answering the sheriff's questions, she asked one of her own. "Are you going to throw me out of the cottage?"

Those blasted mirrored sunglasses stared back at her and she looked away. One one thousand. Two one thousand. If he didn't answer soon she was going to scream. Three one thousand. Four...

"Nope."

Her eyes flew to his face.

"Anybody with eyes in their head can take one look at you and know you're Elizabeth's daughter. You've got a key and nobody seems to be kicking up a fuss that you're there. So for the time being, I'm gonna leave things as they are."

"Thank you, Sheriff. I appreciate that."

"Just don't get too comfortable, Ms. Clarkston. There are too many questions about you and your daddy. And I'm not at all happy about all the trouble cropping up in Promise since you got here. I'm keeping my eye on you, and at the first sign of deception on your part you're on the street and out of my town pronto. Understand?"

Sophie nodded and swallowed the lump in her throat as she watched him walk away.

"Don't let him rattle you, Sophie. I told you before that Sheriff Dalton's bark is a lot worse than his bite." Cain had approached during the end of her conversation with the sheriff and offered her his hand. "Ready to go home?"

Sophie let him pull her to her feet and followed him to the car. The dents along the passenger side made the door hard to open but Cain managed. She slid into the front and fastened her seat belt. As Cain walked around to the driver's side, she glanced at her watch. Almost noon. The day had barely started. She groaned. What else could go wrong today?

"Let's go see my mom," Cain said as he settled behind the wheel.

Sophie squeezed her eyes shut. She had her answer.

"Cain." His mother stepped back, allowing him to enter the house. "What's going on? What's so important you couldn't tell me on the phone? I had to leave my shop in Daisy Lee's hands. Only the good Lord knows what I'll find when I get back. Are you okay?"

Cain stepped into the foyer of the large Colonial and reached an arm behind him to usher Sophie inside. "Mom, this is…"

His mother's eyes locked with hers and she gasped. "Sophia." The older woman's hand flew to her chest and for a split second Sophie wondered if her unannounced appearance had caused her to have a heart attack.

"You're the spitting image of your mother." Martha Garrison stepped back and scrutinized her from head to toe.

Sophie shifted uncomfortably under the inspection. She

glanced at the lilac print wallpaper in the foyer, the large fern in the plant stand at the base of the stairs, the wall of family pictures ascending up the stairwell. She'd never been in a house so opulent. She'd spent most of her life in motels and short-term rentals. Her cottage was the closest thing she'd ever had to a real home. Her eyes soaked in the decor like a sponge.

"You are Elizabeth Weatherly's daughter, aren't you?" The woman's smile reached her eyes.

Sophie found the excitement and friendliness emanating from Cain's mother contagious and took an immediate liking to her. She nodded. "Yes, ma'am."

"And your mother? Is she with you?" Martha pulled the door back farther and peered outside.

"Mom." Cain gently grasped his mother's arm and pulled her back. "Let's go into the living room. We need to talk."

Martha glanced back and forth between them. "Of course, how rude of me. Come in. Make yourself at home." She led the way through the foyer and into a huge, well-lit living room.

Floral arrangements drew Sophie's eyes to the table in front of the bay window and across the room to the mantel above the stone fireplace. Their light scent provided a clean outdoor ambiance to the room. One thing Sophie did recognize was quality woodwork. The plush, cushioned furniture and expensive tables in the room made a statement of quality as well as comfort.

"Can I get anyone a cold drink? Iced tea? Lemonade?"

After they had selected a beverage and were comfortably seated, Martha said, "I'm sorry for my rudeness earlier. But I'm sure I'm not the only one who points out that the resemblance between you and your mother is striking."

Heat seared Sophie's cheeks and she knew she must be lit up like a flashing red beacon. Why was it always so difficult for her to simply socialize like normal people? Why did she always have to feel so awkward and uncomfortable? She hated having these feelings but up to now had lacked the confidence to try and change it. "Thank you, ma'am," she muttered.

"How is your mother? Is she in town with you? I would love to see her."

Cain saved Sophie from answering. "Mom, Elizabeth Weatherly died shortly after Sophie's birth." He smiled at his mother. "That's why we're here. We're hoping you can tell us about her."

"Elizabeth's dead?" Martha's eyes widened. She bowed her head and took a moment to absorb the information. When she spoke again, she addressed Sophie. "Forgive me, my dear. I'm sure my reaction when I first saw you was upsetting."

"Mom, how long has it been since you've been in contact with Elizabeth?" Cain asked.

"Thirty years," his mother answered without hesitation. She smiled warmly at Sophie. "She sent me a brief note announcing your birth. She was so proud of you." Martha sipped her lemonade. "I wanted to write her back. Wanted to send a gift for the baby…um, I mean a gift for you. Unfortunately, Elizabeth didn't include a return address."

"Did you ever hear from her again?" Sophie asked.

"No, child. I'm sorry."

"Thirty years is a long time, Mom," Cain said. "I know you think there's a strong resemblance between Sophie and your friend. But how do you know for sure that Sophie is Elizabeth's daughter?"

Martha's gaze locked with her son's. "Because Elizabeth and I were more than best friends. We grew up together. We were inseparable. I loved her like she was my own sister. Right up to the day she disappeared." She stood up. "Wait right here."

An awkward silence stretched between them when Martha

left the room. Trying to find something to break the silence, Sophie said, "Your mother seems very nice."

Cain clasped her hand. "She's okay as far as mothers go."

She chuckled. Cain might be an expert at many things but hiding his tender feelings for his mom wasn't one of them. Sophie sighed. How would her life have been different if her mother hadn't died? Would they still have traveled constantly or would her mother have insisted on settling down? Would she have been able to attend school, meet other children, make friends?

Immediately immersed in guilt, Sophie tried to stop her errant thoughts. She was being selfish. Her father had done the best he could. He was a single parent…of a girl, no less… and he didn't always get it right. He hadn't known the first thing about makeup or party dresses. He hadn't given a second thought to his daughter wanting to attend school dances or to date.

He had never realized how many hundreds of times Sophie needed the advice, comfort or leadership of another female. A bittersweet smile tugged the corner of her mouth when she remembered the many nights she'd cried herself to sleep, missing the mother she didn't remember.

Martha Garrison carried a shoe box into the room, deposited it on the cocktail table and gingerly removed the lid as if she was opening a secret treasure. She lifted out old greeting cards, letters, scraps of paper, a few pictures and then she smiled. "Here it is." She withdrew a card yellowed with age and handed it to Sophie.

"It's the last correspondence I ever had with your mother. I've kept it all these years…right in here with all my other life treasures…." She patted the box on the table. "Just in case. I never gave up hope I'd hear from her again."

Martha picked up the box and cradled it on her lap. "And

now her daughter is sitting in front of me and I..." The older woman's eyes misted. "I feel like someone rolled back the clock and your mother is here again exactly as I remember her."

Sophie squirmed and lowered her gaze to the card. She didn't have a clue what she should say or how she should act under the circumstances. Her fingers trembled as she gently ran them over the outside of the birth announcement. Her birth announcement. Written in her mother's hand. How surreal this all was—the last two weeks felt like a dream and no matter how hard she tried she just couldn't wake up.

Cain gently took the card from her fingers. His eyes held empathy and understanding. "Let's look at it together, okay?"

He opened the card. It was a typical birth announcement. Name. Date. Weight. Significantly missing were the parents' names or any other identifying items such as hospital or home address. At the bottom of the card was a note in handwritten script.

I couldn't let the happiest day of my life pass and not share it with my dearest friend, the sister of my heart. I miss you so much. I hope you are happy (and that you and 'the one' are still together. That way there'll be a happy-ever-after for both of us). I'm sorry I haven't been in touch. And I'm sorry I can't let you know where I am. Maybe someday I can. But know that I think of you every day of my life and I miss you.
Elizabeth

Silence engulfed the room. Cain broke it when he looked up at his mother. "The one?"

Martha grinned, "Your father, of course. Elizabeth and

I had a code name for him so we could talk about him in his presence without him knowing it." His mother laughed. "One of Elizabeth's ideas. It worked pretty well, too. Your father would squint his eyes and glare at me suspiciously, but he never knew for sure we were talking about him so he wouldn't say anything."

Sophie took the card back from Cain and addressed his mother. "Why couldn't she tell you where she was? What happened between the two of you?"

"A man. That's what happened." Martha's mouth pulled into a grimace.

"Maybe your daddy was somebody else. I certainly hope so."

Sophie inhaled sharply.

"Mom!"

"I'm sorry. I shouldn't have said that. I'm sure the man who caused your mother to leave after her high school graduation isn't your father. This announcement came six years after she left. I'm certain she came to her senses and married somebody else. I'm doubly sure because she sounds so happy in this note."

"What happened, Mom? Who was the guy and why did Elizabeth leave Promise?"

"She left because her grandfather had demanded she stop seeing him. And she wasn't about to stop. She was in love. Foolish. Stupid. But in love."

"Why did her grandfather oppose the match? Was he a teenager from the wrong side of the tracks?"

"He was no teenager. Elizabeth was the teenager. She was only seventeen and just finished her senior year. He was in his late twenties. Maybe early thirties. He's lucky her grandfather didn't have him arrested. Probably would have if he had found out soon enough. But the night after he laid down the law, Elizabeth ran off."

Sophie mentally calculated the age difference between her mother and father and knew the man was most likely her father.

"But the age wasn't the thing that had everyone all upset. After all, Elizabeth was going to be eighteen in a couple of weeks, making her an adult. Her grandfather wouldn't have had a legal leg to stand on," Mrs. Garrison continued. "It was the other thing everyone worried about."

"What other thing?" Cain asked.

"Federal agents were looking for him. He was a criminal."

TEN

Sophie hitched a breath. "That's not true. My father never committed a criminal act in his life. He's a good man. Kind. Compassionate. He begins every morning of his life reading the Bible and praying."

Cain reached over and clasped her hand. "Sophie, calm down. I know this is hard for you to hear…."

She pulled her hand away and jumped to her feet. "It's not hard to hear if you want to waste your time listening to lies. I'm telling you it's not true."

"I'm sorry," Mrs. Garrison said. "I should have chosen my words with more discretion. Besides, dear, I'm sure we're not talking about the same man anyway. I didn't hear from your mother for six years after she left town. If your father was the decent, Christian man you describe, I'm sure your mother met someone else…not the man this town knew."

Sophie glared at Cain's mother. Pain and anger consumed her. "You *are* talking about my father, Mrs. Garrison. And I don't appreciate the gossip you're spreading about him. My dad never broke the law. He never even had a parking ticket."

Cain wrapped his arm around Sophie's shoulders, settled her back down on her chair and crouched down until he was at eye level with her. "Sophie." He clasped her hand and locked his gaze with hers. "Try to be patient. Let my mother tell us what she knows." He waved a hand to halt her immediate protest. "Or what she thinks she knows."

Sophie pulled her hand away, withdrew a square of clay from her pants pocket and folded her hands in her lap, her fingers furiously squeezing and releasing the clay. "She's wrong, Cain. My dad wouldn't break the law."

"Sophie…" The deep tenor of his voice raced along her nerve endings and lowered to a soothing rumble. "I need you to think for a minute. Think about the contents of your father's tool box."

The blood drained from her face. Her fingers froze. The fake IDs. Lies. Deception. What did she really know about her father? And in that instant she released the breath she'd been holding. Her shoulders slumped in defeat. Did she want to know the truth? Was she strong enough to learn it? She looked into Cain's eyes. His empathy and compassion was almost her undoing. She nodded and turned her attention back to Mrs. Garrison.

"I'm sorry. I didn't mean to upset you." The woman chewed the bottom of her lip exactly the way Cain did when he was upset or concentrating and Sophie smiled in spite of herself. Cain sat back down and took control of the conversation.

"Mom, you didn't do anything wrong. It's just that this news is a bit shocking for Sophie. Her father disappeared without a trace a little more than two weeks ago. She's asked me to help her find him. Anything you know, anything at all, will be a help."

Mrs. Garrison put her fingers to her face. "But what if Sophie's right? What if my information is wrong, nothing more than town gossip? After all, I never met the man. Elizabeth kept her relationship a secret almost to the very end… even from me, her best friend."

Sophie saw a light sheen in Martha Garrison's eyes. She'd

been hurt when her mother had left town, and it was eviden⸱ some of those feelings were still alive and well.

"Even bad information can be helpful, Mom," Cain assured her. "At least it will help close another door." Cain settled back in his chair and crossed an ankle over his knee. "Star⸱ at the beginning. Tell us everything you know."

Martha glanced at Sophie, offered a timid smile and the⸱ turned her attention to her son. "I can't be sure but I thin⸱ Elizabeth met him during summer break from school. I start⸱ ed to notice a change in her. We used to hang out together al⸱ the time and suddenly she wasn't available. She kept makin⸱ one excuse after another about why she couldn't meet me fo⸱ a swim or take in a movie or just hang out."

Martha sipped her iced tea. A frown creased her forehead "In the beginning I accepted her lame excuses that her grand⸱ father needed her to run an errand or do an extra chore. I eve⸱ believed her when she said she'd taken a part-time job, eve⸱ though she never did tell me where." Her weak laugh hel⸱ no humor. "She saw me just enough to keep me from askin⸱ too many questions, but I knew something had changed.

"Elizabeth was always outgoing, optimistic, but suddenl⸱ things seemed different, more intense. She was happy, reall⸱ happy. Her eyes sparkled. She smiled all the time. And I'⸱ catch her sitting by herself gazing into the distance like sh⸱ was enjoying a secret only she knew. In retrospect, she acte⸱ like someone in love.

"So one day down by the pond…matter of fact, I'm prett⸱ sure it was the same day I took that picture…we were picnick⸱ ing by the water. The other two girls were in the water an⸱ Elizabeth and I were lying in the sun. I asked her point-blan⸱ if she was seeing anyone. She swore me to secrecy and spille⸱ the beans."

"What did she say?" Sophie asked.

Martha stared at her for several seconds and then said

"She told me that she'd met the love of her life. That he was a wonderful man and she'd never been happier."

Martha dropped her gaze and took another sip of her tea. "I was a teenager myself back then. I hate to admit it, but I was jealous. Someone was taking my place with my best friend and I wasn't happy about it." Martha smiled. "But when I saw how happy this guy made her, I was ready to try to accept him."

Cain leaned forward, the tenseness in his body claiming Sophie's attention. "What was his name, Mom?"

"I don't remember."

"What?" Sophie couldn't hide her disappointment. "How could you forget his name? And why did you think he was a criminal?"

Martha folded her hands in her lap and looked directly at Sophie. "Honey, I was seventeen years old. I don't have to tell you that was several decades ago. Elizabeth and I only talked about him that one time. She left town the next day and I never saw her again. I'm sorry. I really am."

Sophie felt the sincerity behind Mrs. Garrison's words.

"And the criminal part?" Cain frowned at his mother.

"Two federal marshals showed up in Promise and asked Sheriff Dalton, not Roy Dalton but his daddy, James, the whereabouts of this man. Everyone knows federal marshals don't look for law-abiding citizens. They look for criminals."

"A criminal?" Sophie could barely squeeze the words from her throat. Her breathing tightened and she found herself fighting for breath.

Dad? Her dad? Could it be?

"When the news started flying around town, Elizabeth ran away. Old man Weatherly called out the biggest manhunt for the two of them that the town had ever seen. Searched every house, every building, every inch on the mountains and through the woods. Put Elizabeth's picture on the news. Even posted a reward for any information helping to find her."

Martha's fingers trembled as they smoothed the fabric of her skirt. She chewed her lip with such force, Sophie expected to see blood. "No one heard from Elizabeth again." She tilted her head and smiled lovingly at Sophie. "Until the day I received that birth announcement." She leaned forward and gently stroked Sophie's hand. "She was so proud of you…and so, so happy." She leaned back in her chair. "You really are the spitting image of her, you know." She sighed and lifted the yellowed card in her fingers. "When I received this, I knew we were still best friends. I believed I'd hear from her again soon. But I never did."

Sophie's insides churned with mixed emotions. The woman sitting in front of her had known her mother since birth, had been best friends with her, had cried for her when she left, had missed her enough to keep her one and only card with all her family treasures. She wondered what it must be like to have a best friend. To have someone to share secrets with, laugh with, trust. Someone to whisper to about those special feelings of first love. Her mother may have died young but, based on everything she'd been told about her, she'd had a rich, wonderful life. And, although happy for her mother, Sophie couldn't help but wish she'd had the opportunity to form some of those relationships herself.

Cain stood and offered a hand to Sophie, helping her to her feet. "Thanks, Mom. I really appreciate it."

"Yes, Mrs. Garrison. Thank you. I'm sorry about the way I reacted earlier."

"Sophie, I would have reacted the exact same way. I just wish I could have been more helpful."

"We've got to go now, Mom. I've got a few leads to follow up and I have to get Sophie home before I do."

"Are you staying at the Weatherly place?"

Sophie nodded.

"Please visit again and join me for tea. I'll tell you quite a few stories about the shenanigans your mother and I pulled on your grandfather out there."

Sophie smiled at the woman. "I'd like that very much. Thank you."

When they reached the front door, they could hear Cain's mother behind them. "It started with a *B,* or maybe a *G.*"

Cain turned. "Mom?"

"Ohh, I'm just so mad at myself. I know that name's on the tip of my tongue and I just can't catch it." Her eyes lit with excitement and she snapped her fingers. "I know. I'm going to have your father bring down my old high school boxes from the attic. I kept a journal back then. I bet I wrote his name down in one of the journals."

"Do you want me to go up and get them?"

"No. No." She waved Cain away. "Your father and I will do it together. It won't hurt us to sit in the attic and go down memory lane together. Good for the soul." She winked at Cain and waved on.

"Call me, Mom, if you find the name."

"Of course."

They walked to the car in silence. Cain held open the passenger door and Sophie slid inside. He settled behind the steering wheel and neither said a word until he'd pulled out into traffic.

"Don't take me home."

Cain lifted an eyebrow.

"I'm going to your office with you. I'm good with computers. I'll help you do your research."

"Sophie, I think you…"

"Don't argue with me, Cain. I'm going with you."

Cain sighed and turned his attention back to the road. He knew better than to argue with an angry woman.

* * *

Cain stopped abruptly in the hallway. He held his finger to his lips for silence and pushed Sophie gently against the wall. He eased his Glock out of the back of his belt and gestured for her to remain where she was. Stealthily, he moved toward his office door.

He wrapped the fingers of his left hand around the door-knob and was just about to turn it when the door flew open and it was all he could do not to fall flat on his face.

"Tell me you have a permit for that gun, son." Sheriff Dalton stood in the doorway, both fists on his hips.

Cain slid the gun back into his belt and straightened up. "Of course, I have a permit. Tell *me* that you know breaking and entering is a crime."

Sheriff Dalton snorted. "Ain't a crime, boy, if the waiting room door to your office is open." He stood back and gestured both of them inside. "Better talk to that sister of yours if you want to keep people out of the office when you're away. I saw her hightailing it to the diner right before I walked in. Obviously, she didn't lock up."

Cain made a mental note to do exactly that.

"What can I do for you, Sheriff?" Cain asked. He sat down in one of the leather chairs in front of his desk. Sophie claimed the other chair, which left the sheriff standing in the doorway.

"You got it backward. It's what I can do for you." The large man crossed to Cain's desk, retrieved a folder and handed it to Sophie.

"Your father's real name is Dominic Gimmelli, sole heir of Vincent Gimmelli, the head of a Mafia crime family doing business in Maryland with heavy New York ties. He married your mother, Elizabeth Weatherly, six years before you were born. A copy of their marriage certificate is inside."

Sophie paled but otherwise showed no reaction to the sheriff's words. She opened the folder and pulled out the document he referred to, as well as dozens of local newspaper clippings.

"Your parents were front-page news in Promise for weeks. First, because Elizabeth ran off with your dad. And then the papers had a field day when they discovered just who your daddy was."

Tears glistened in Sophie's eyes and her fingers trembled as she gingerly lifted one clipping after another.

"Do you know where her father is now, Sheriff?" Cain tried unsuccessfully to hide the hopeful note in his own voice.

"No. But I wish I did. I've got a few questions I'd like to ask him."

Sophie squared her shoulders and, when she spoke, her voice was calm and collected. "Thank you, Sheriff Dalton. I appreciate your finding this information for me."

The sheriff stared at her long and hard. "I assumed your father died years ago. Seems to me a lot of other people thought so, too. Obviously, I was wrong. I'm hoping your recent troubles have nothing to do with your father. But, make no mistake, little lady, I won't be a happy camper if you've brought organized crime into my town."

Without a word, he turned and stormed out of the office.

Sophie's eyes looked bleak as she met Cain's gaze. "Well, at least now I know who I really am." Her grin was bittersweet. "A Mafia princess."

ELEVEN

The past two days had been filled with nothing but dead ends and disappointments. Sophie, each hand holding a cup of hot coffee, pushed the porch door open with her hip. She sat down on the top step, nodded to Cain, who was rummaging through files in a box in his trunk, and placed his cup on the step beside her.

The two of them had researched every false identity they'd pulled from her father's tool box, only to discover he'd only used the IDs just as long as their stay in those towns.

The biggest lead had been the old newspaper clippings Sheriff Dalton had given them. Her father had turned out to be the son of a notorious capo of a Maryland crime family. From everything they'd read in the papers, there had been no evidence implicating her father in the family business. His only tie to the Mob seemed to be his lineage.

They assumed Elizabeth had met her dad at the local college. Dominic Gimmelli had been a visiting art instructor for a summer session. Records showed Elizabeth had signed up for one of his courses.

No one knew what the federal marshals wanted with Dominic. Cain hadn't even been able to prove federal marshals had ever shown up in town at all. But rumor of their arrival had been the catalyst that had caused Elizabeth and Dominic to run off together. Shortly after their marriage, all records of Dominic and Elizabeth Gimmelli had vanished.

Sophia Joy Gimmelli. The name slid off her tongue like something lifted from an Italian film. Daughter of Elizabeth Weatherly and Dominic Gimmelli. Sophie hoped speaking the words aloud would make them feel real. It didn't. In her heart she was Sophia Joy Clarkston, that's who she would always be. Someday she'd wake up and find she'd had the nightmare to end all nightmares. Someday.

The sound of a trunk lid slamming shut pulled her thoughts back to the present. She smiled and watched Cain approach. Today his limp was barely discernible.

He plopped down on the step beside her and raised his cup in a faux toast. "Thanks, I needed this."

"Long night last night?"

"Yeah. I had to finish the paperwork on two other cases and then Holly called. One of her cooks was out sick and she commandeered my services."

"Somehow I can't picture you in an apron and a chef's hat."

"Ahh, but you seem to enjoy the results of my labor. If I recall, you had seconds of my pot roast the other night."

Sophie laughed. "True, which reminds me, you have to give me your recipe."

Cain placed a hand over his heart and feigned shock. "No way are you getting the recipe out of me. A master chef never reveals his secret ingredients."

"No way, huh?" Sophie leaned closer and teasingly batted her eyelashes at him. When her skin brushed against his, a shiver danced along her spine. Her heart fluttered in her chest. Her breathing quickened.

Instead of drawing back, she leaned closer, mesmerized by these tantalizing feelings and unable to turn away. She whispered, her voice soft, tender, "No way at all?"

Her unexpected flirting surprised them both and the air crackled with awareness. The darkened intensity in Cain's eyes took her breath away. Sophie panicked and started to move away.

"Don't." Cain caught her forearm and held her close. The hint of his aftershave teased her; the warmth of his breath fanned her face.

"Sophie?"

His voice held a depth she'd never heard before, an unspoken question that hung in the air between them. His lips paused mere inches from hers. Her eyes locked with his.

Cain lowered his head and his lips captured hers…gently, softly and then with a promise of something more.

Sophie kissed back, her pulse racing, her blood rushing through her body like white-water rapids, as if she were on the adventure of her life.

Just as abruptly as it had begun, the moment ended. Cain had pulled away. Seconds of silence beat between them. Sophie placed her fingertips against her lips, not knowing if she was sorry the kiss had ended or thankful one of the two of them had come to their senses.

"Sophie, I'm—"

She shot a look at him. "Don't you dare insult me with an apology."

He grinned that cocky, lopsided grin she'd learned to love and held his hands up defensively. "No, ma'am. Wouldn't think of it."

He turned sideways on the step, subtly putting some distance between them, and leaned his back against the porch post. "I'm not sorry I kissed you. I've been wondering what your lips were like from the first moment you walked into my office." His brown eyes caught and held hers. "And they're just as sweet as I imagined they'd be."

An embarrassed flush rushed through her body and Sophie

knew the telltale coloring of her cheeks and throat exposed her true feelings.

"But…" He lifted his coffee cup, took a sip, and then said, "It was selfish…and unprofessional…and I won't let it happen again."

She nodded, keeping her eyes turned away. "Sounds like a plan…a good one if you ask me."

Cain chuckled but refrained from saying anything more.

Sophie couldn't believe what she had done. She'd never openly flirted with anyone before. Sure, she'd been kissed a few times. But she'd never experienced a kiss so powerful, so full of emotion, so confusing.

After a few moments of companionable silence, Sophie decided that if she'd dared to be flirtatious, maybe she could be bold as well. She had nothing left to lose. She'd already made a fool of herself once today. And there were things she wanted to know. Questions that burned to be asked. She turned her attention to Cain. "I noticed you're barely limping today."

"Yeah." He glanced at his leg. "I haven't been sliding across asphalt for a few days or sitting with it cramped in a car for hours. When I treat it right, it returns the favor."

Sophie smiled and then pressed on with what she really wanted to know. "How did you get hurt?"

"On the job." His clipped words let her know he didn't intend to discuss it further, which piqued her curiosity even more.

He knew everything there was to know about her and she knew so little about him. He was a professional and good at his job. She'd met his family, seen him interact with them and with other people in the town, knew he was kind, intelligent, compassionate. But that was surface stuff, the kinds of things he'd reveal to anyone. The deeper things—the secret, painful things that happen to us and make us the people we become—he managed to keep those things hidden.

She knew it was none of her business. She didn't have a right to question him about his personal life. But she couldn't help herself. She was drawn to this man on a deep, emotional level. She found herself experiencing feelings she had never had before for anyone. The more she knew the more she wanted to know. So she pushed.

"How long were you a cop?"

"Seven years."

"Was your injury the reason you left the force?"

His lips pulled into a straight line. For a moment, she thought he wasn't going to answer her. "I'm not the kind of guy to be happy spending the rest of my days sitting behind a desk." He tapped his thigh. "And I couldn't trust my leg enough to bank a partner's life on it working when I needed it to."

"So you left the force..."

He nodded but offered nothing more.

"You miss it, don't you?"

He spun his legs down to the next step. His grim expression reminded her of carved granite, a shrug his only answer to her question.

Sophie figured, she'd gone this far, she might as well push a little harder. She inched over on the top step and gently placed a hand on his shoulder. "Tell me about it."

He glanced at her, mixed emotions struggling in his eyes. "Sophie, it was a long time ago. What does it matter now?"

"Please."

Silence stretched so long between them she thought he wouldn't respond. The sound of his voice startled her.

"I made a mistake...an almost fatal mistake...and it cost me."

When he didn't go any further, Sophie drew in a deep breath and asked, "What did you do?"

"I got personally involved with a woman on a case I was working. She betrayed me."

The anguish in his voice froze her breath in her throat. She remained stock-still, her hand still resting on his shoulder, her expression as calm as she could keep it as she waited for him to continue.

Cain sighed deeply, all the air leaving his body, all the hesitation and the pain mingling with it.

"I worked undercover in narcotics. It was easy at first. I was young. Eager. Made it easy for me to fit in."

A cloud crossed his expression.

"Sophie, none of this matters…." His voice trailed off.

"Yes, Cain, it does."

His eyes met hers.

"It matters to me. It helps me understand who you were… and how you came to be who you are now."

He drew a long gulp of coffee, set his mug down and stood up. He leaned against the porch railing and stared into the distance. His shoulders slumped. He sighed audibly. And then he started to speak…and didn't stop until he'd told her everything.

"I made friends, best friends with one of the dealers. His name was Joey Petrone…and he had a sister named Lucy."

Sophie's breath hitched at the pain she saw reflected in his eyes but she didn't dare interrupt.

He drew his hands down his face. "It's a thin line when you're undercover. You've got to build relationships, build trust with the dealers. You do that by building a reputation, a persona that bears no reflection on your real life.

"You're acting. Living some made-up character's life. Hanging with them. Bonding with the dealers. And as you move into their world you become more isolated from your own, from the force…from the person you really are, until it becomes hard—sometimes really hard—to remember where you drew that line between one world and the other."

Sophie listened in fascination, intrigued by his words but afraid of where the story would lead.

"Joey, Lucy and I became the neighborhood threesome. Wherever you saw one of us, you saw the other two." A bittersweet smile twisted his lips. "And I committed the ultimate sin…. I began to believe I was this other guy, lived in this other world, dared to fall in love with this other woman."

His voice cracked.

The twilight wrapped around them and the sound of frogs and crickets filled the air.

"There wasn't church in that other world…or prayer…or God. And at that time in my life, it didn't matter. All that mattered was Lucy."

Cain looked at Sophie. Evening shadows fell across his face. Still she could read his doubt, his reluctance to remember, but he continued just as he'd promised he would.

"Lucy was a drug addict who couldn't keep clean. No matter how much I tried to help her. No matter how many times she promised she would."

His voice became empty, hollow.

"I loved her. And when she discovered I was an undercover cop, she protected my cover…because she loved me back."

Even in the dusk, Sophie could see a lone tear slide down his cheek.

"But she couldn't let herself love me more than the dope. Couldn't love me enough to pass up the opportunity for a quick fix when I wouldn't supply her with any more money, and all she had left to trade was me. So she did.

"Joey got the dealers, normally in competition with each other but united in this, to band together to make an example out of me. They didn't put a gun to my head and make it clean and easy. No. They tortured me. They beat me. When they were done, there was barely a bone in my body that hadn't been shattered.

"Then they dragged me in an alley and threw me like a piece of garbage beside a Dumpster."

Cain's voice was nothing more now than a harsh whisper.

"They dumped me in a filthy, rat-infested alley and left me to die…with Lucy." He choked on a sob. "She was already dead from an overdose."

Cain shrugged. "I don't know how long I laid there, drifting in and out of consciousness, in and out of a sea of unbearable pain. A homeless man found us and told a cop."

He looked at Sophie and his eyes looked desolate, empty. "There were dark days when I'd wished I hadn't been found. When both the emotional and physical pain seemed more than I could bear.

"I needed several plastic surgery operations to return my face to a semblance of the person I used to be. Someone who didn't make his father cringe and his mother weep. Not including the countless operations I endured to fix all the other broken bones. The casts. The physical therapy five days a week so I could learn to walk again.

"They fixed it all. It took over a year and a half but they fixed everything. Except for my heart…" He stared right at her. "Nobody seems to be able to fix my heart. The affair with Lucy almost cost me my life, and it did cost Lucy hers. It cost me my career. And it cost me my belief in human beings. I haven't ever been able to trust anyone on that level since then."

Cain faced her. "I hope I've answered all your questions, Sophie. Are you happy now?" His expression of raw pain and torment seized her heart. Without another word he strode to the car, got in and drove away.

She stared at the trail of dust he'd left in his wake, tears sliding down her cheeks. As painful as it had been for Cain to tell his story and Sophie to hear it, she wasn't sorry she'd asked. She felt even closer to him now. They shared a common bond. She knew all about pain and broken trust.

She carried the empty mugs inside and locked the doors. All she could think about while she washed the few dishes in the sink was Cain. He shouldn't be driving as upset as he was. He shouldn't be alone after reliving those horrible memories. She wanted to throw her arms around him and hold him close. She wanted to cry with him, comfort him, be with him.

The phone rang.

Cain.

She grabbed it before the second ring. "Cain?"

"We ain't waitin' no longer. Give us back what's ours or die."

TWELVE

Sophie drove her car down the dirt path and toward the main road to town. Five days had passed since Cain had driven away on this same stretch of road and left on a business trip. Five days of crisp, clipped telephone calls from him, checking in, making sure she was safe, but keeping his distance. Five days of visits from Holly, who insisted on sleeping on Sophie's sofa every night to appease Cain. Visits from Mrs. Garrison bringing banana bread or homemade soup. Five days since Sophie had been able to hear a phone ring without jumping out of her skin.

She didn't know how to handle the threatening phone call she'd received. She wanted to tell Cain—but he was purposely keeping his distance and she didn't want him to feel obligated to her in any way. She didn't feel comfortable telling Holly or Mrs. Garrison. She was still trying to overcome her shyness and form a relationship with them. Telling them she'd received a telephone call threatening to kill her didn't seem like the best way to do that. And, of course, she considered telling Sheriff Dalton—only about a thousand times a day. But it had been one telephone call. One. Nothing had come of it. None followed it. So, no, it didn't feel right to tell the sheriff—not yet.

So five days had passed since Cain had left on his "business trip." And no one knew when he'd return. Five days that passed so slowly she swore she could hear the seconds tick on the clock.

But, if she was being honest, not all the time had crawled by.

Sophie had wished she could have made the visits with Cain's mother last longer. As they sat on the porch sharing a cup of tea, she found herself hanging on to her every word, eager to hear the stories Martha told her that brought her own mother to life. And she couldn't forget the evenings with Holly, who was becoming her first true friend. She'd laughed so hard her stomach ached as Holly shared stories of some of her childhood antics.

Even joining Cain's family for Sunday church service had been both a hurdle…and a joy. The family believed and practiced their belief. It made Sophie question what she really believed. Sometimes she thought God was only for people too weak to deal with life on their own. Other times a small voice inside whispered that if she would just open the door to her heart, even just a crack, she'd find the truth and the truth would be everything she'd ever hoped and more.

As much as Sophie wished the time spent with Cain's family hadn't flown by, in other ways time hadn't passed fast enough. Her father was still missing. Cain was no closer to finding the truth. And now she jumped sky-high every time she heard a phone ring.

The car hit a pothole. The abrupt bouncing jarred the steering wheel in her hands and brought her mind to the task at hand and away from her constant thoughts of Cain. The top of her head hit the ceiling, which wouldn't have happened if she'd remembered to lock her seat belt in place before she'd left. She rubbed her head and then slowed the vehicle and struggled with the strap until she heard the familiar click. Breathing a sigh of relief, she vowed to get her head out of the clouds and pay attention. Reaching up to adjust her rearview mirror, she noted a dark sedan about a hundred yards behind her.

Alarm slithered up her spine but she dismissed it. After all, this was the main highway. Of course, there'd be other vehicles on the road. But her cottage was far enough from town that she didn't usually see anyone else coming or going until she'd driven closer to town.

She tried to pay attention to the road in front of her but her eyes kept darting to the mirror. The car behind her wasn't doing anything threatening. The driver wasn't speeding or driving too close. It hung back about a hundred yards and didn't seem to be in any hurry at all.

Still…an ominous discomfort knotted her stomach and gooseflesh pimpled her arms.

Maybe she should have listened to Holly and ridden into town with her this morning. But Sophie had had errands to run, the grocery store topping the list, and she needed her own transportation.

Stop being so paranoid. So there's another car on the road. So what?

Sophie flipped on the radio and tried to relax. A favorite song filled the air and she tapped her fingers on the steering wheel to the beat of the music. She would not let her overactive imagination get the better of her. She forced herself to keep her eyes on the road ahead.

One mile.

Three miles.

She couldn't stand it another second. Her gaze flew to the mirror and she gasped. The car was right on her tail, ten, maybe twelve feet behind.

A black sedan. Just like the one that had tried to force Cain and her off the road.

Her pulse points throbbed and her heart pounded against her chest.

She squinted her eyes and stared hard at the mirrored reflection. Two men sat in the front seat. The one in the passenger seat seemed stocky, possibly bald. The driver definitely had a beard. These weren't teenagers out for a joyride…not that anyone ever believed it had been teenagers before. Why was this happening? Who were these people and what did they want with her?

Sophie's foot hit the accelerator and her car lurched forward. Only a few more minutes and she'd be approaching Main Street, which meant people, businesses and safety. She fumbled inside the pocket of her purse and pulled out her cell phone. Her thumb slid across the preprogrammed 911 button but she didn't place the call. What would she tell the dispatcher? *I'm driving down the highway toward town and a car is behind me.* Yeah, right.

Her eyes darted to the mirror and her heart almost leapt from her chest. The black sedan hugged her bumper, no more than a foot between them now. She had a clear view of the man behind the wheel. Black eyes glared back at her. Soulless eyes.

Keep your cool. You're not stupid. You can handle this. You just need to calm down and think.

She took a deep breath and tried to gain control of her runaway emotions. She couldn't help but think this would be a great time to offer up a quick prayer. But just as quickly as the thought entered her head, she dismissed it. Hadn't she spent most of her childhood years praying for her father to remarry so she would have a mother? And through her teenage years hadn't she begged God for a friend to end her loneliness? Then when her father disappeared hadn't she begged, pleaded, bargained—anything and everything she could think of—to have her dad come back? But why had she bothered? God never answered her prayers.

Just ahead, Main Street stretched before her like a welcome runway for a troubled airliner. She took a deep breath and began to release the pressure on the accelerator. Her car slowed.

The car behind her slowed in tandem.

She had to be absolutely certain she was being followed. What if this was merely a man in a black car driving into town? She didn't want to make a fool of herself. The sheriff already had strong doubts about her character. She slowed the car even more and turned down the first side street she reached.

The car stayed behind her.

She made a quick left.

When the black sedan followed, Sophie knew exactly what to do. Without hesitation she drove directly to Sheriff Dalton's and pulled into a spot right beside a patrol car. The sedan continued past, made a left and disappeared.

Sophie sat in the car, her eyes glued to the street where the sedan had turned. When it was obvious it wasn't going to make a reappearance, she let herself breathe. Her arms trembled and her pulse continued to race but gradually she began to calm down.

The license plate number! Why hadn't she looked at it when the car had driven by? What was the matter with her?

She'd been scared to death, that's what...but proud of herself, too. She'd kept her head and hadn't panicked. Should she report the incident to the sheriff? What could she tell him? A black sedan followed her into town and then kept on going when she stopped. He'd think she was crazy...if he didn't already.

Cain.

He'd believe her. He'd understand.

But he was away on business. Was it really business or did he need a few days to get away from her? A deep sadness enveloped her when she realized her pushy curiosity might have come with a price tag she didn't want to pay.

Sophie accepted the beads from one of Martha Garrison's students and realized her hands had stopped trembling. She glanced at the parking lot for the hundredth time in the past two hours…still no black sedan. Maybe she'd been wrong about this morning's incident. Maybe she hadn't been followed and the anger in the driver's eyes had been there simply because she was in his way.

Maybe.

Her eyes skimmed the parking lot again. Still no black sedan. She relaxed and turned her attention back to the class. Martha, sitting at a table across the room, helped some of the teenagers slice their multicolored clay ropes and shape them into jewelry beads ready to be baked. She glanced up and smiled.

"Look at my necklace, Ms. Clarkston. It's a one-of-a-kind and I made it all by myself."

The misshapen beads and mottled colors didn't seem to bother the girl at all. "You're right, Kelly. That is definitely a one-of-a-kind. Congratulations."

Sophie returned the child's smile and watched her flit from table to table showing her necklace to the other kids. Her craft idea had been a big hit today with a majority of the teenagers. Warmth filled her and she couldn't help feeling a sense of pride. It felt good helping others. Really good.

Her gaze wandered the room and locked on a belligerent teenage boy in the back of the classroom refusing to participate. She recognized him. He was the same boy Sheriff Dalton had arrested that night outside Holly's. She took a good long look at him and realized he wasn't eighteen or

nineteen as she'd first assumed. This was merely a boy...
fourteen...fifteen at best. Drag racing someone's car? Wow.
Where were his parents? Maybe that was the problem.

Martha frequently talked about the dysfunctional homes
most of these kids came from. She tried to make a positive
impact on the young tweens and teenagers. She tried to edu-
cate them on options other than a life of crime. She did her
best to introduce them to a God who had big plans for their
lives, who would love them and be their strength, no matter
what.

Sophie found herself dwelling on Martha's words. A God
who would stand beside you no matter what the problem...
strengthen you...fill you with peace...and joy. What would
that be like? Sophie had always believed in God because her
father had taught God's existence as fact, just as emphatically
and naturally as she'd been taught her colors.

This is blue, Sophie. Deep, dark blue. She could hear her
father's voice in her mind just as clearly as if he was standing right beside her. *Paint it on a canvas and it becomes a
midnight sky or a stormy sea. But, ahh, Sophie, mix in just
a little bit of white and what do you get? A lighter blue. The
color of the sky on a cloudless day. But still the color blue.
God has an endless palette, Sophie, and He made it all for
us.*

She sighed. Was it really that easy? Her father's faith?
God, ever present both in stormy and cloudless skies? After
a lifetime of her father's example and now seeing how Cain's
family lived their faith, she was beginning to understand that
each individual comes face-to-face at some point in their
lives with having to define what they believe for themselves,
having to decide whether the focus of their lives belonged to
the Lord...or not.

So, what did she believe?

She remembered many mornings sitting in the sun and

reading her mother's Bible. Clasping her father's hand as they bowed their heads in prayer before their meals. She remembered talking to God…all the time…as if He could hear every word. And she remembered life being peaceful… and content…and safe.

When had her feelings changed?

She didn't have to ponder that question. The day her father had disappeared. The day she'd begged and pleaded for God to turn back the clock…to perform a miracle and change her life…give her a mother who hadn't died…give her a father who hadn't left. Her faith had faded side by side with hope, making her wonder if she had ever had true faith at all.

An overwhelming sense of sadness cloaked her like a heavy coat. She felt confused, depressed, alone. She'd give anything to feel God at her side…to know He'd never leave her even when others had…to feel the joy and peace she had known before. But all she felt was empty and hollow. God didn't seem to be at her side anymore.

But for the first time in weeks, her anger had lessened enough for her to be able to hear a soft voice inside her head. A niggling conscience that kept asking her who had turned away from whom?

Her eyes lit again on the young boy in the back of the room. He seemed to be far away from God at the moment, too. His sullen expression and "I could care less" body language couldn't hide the hint of interest she saw in his eyes when he watched the other teens.

Slowly, she walked toward him. As she passed the other tables, she glanced at the students' projects. One boy had created an intricate tile design that he planned to attach to a leather wristband. Another sculpted a skull and worked securing it to leather straps. Her lips twitched in amusement. Somehow Sophie didn't think this was exactly the type of jewelry Mrs. Garrison had had in mind, but at least the teenagers were here in class and not causing trouble on the streets.

As she approached the back of the room, she saw the boy stiffen and turn away but she didn't let his hostile body language discourage her. She homed in like a heat-seeking missile to its target.

"Hi." She grinned and perched a hip on the edge of his table.

He shot her a halfhearted glare and didn't respond.

"You're Jimmy Falcon, aren't you?"

"A-plus for the teacher," he sneered. Sophie almost laughed out loud. He was trying so hard to be a tough guy…and failing miserably.

"Not interested in the class?"

"Why should I be? Only wimps wear jewelry. Do I look like a wimp to you?" His eyes baited her.

Sophie bit her bottom lip so hard she thought she'd draw blood. She couldn't let him know how humorous she found him, even if he was the cutest, non-frightening punk she'd ever met.

"Clay is an art form only limited by the imagination and creativity of the artist," she said as she picked up a block from the table and kneaded it.

"Yeah, right. Whatever."

"If you're not interested in jewelry, perhaps sculpting a figure would be more your speed."

Jimmy cocked an eyebrow. Interest and doubt flashed through his eyes but he remained silent.

Sophie slid off the table, gathered some of her tools and sat down beside him. A short time later, with the help of her scalpel and garlic press, she placed a miniature sheep in front of him.

"That's an example of one of the pieces I made for a Nativity scene I sculpted for my father last Christmas." She picked up the piece and held it gingerly in the palm of her hand. She remembered how much her father had loved the gift. He'd even crafted a stable to house all her miniature figurines and decided to display them year-round, not just for Christmas. Her heart swelled with pain. She missed him so much.

"Yeah, I get it. Jewelry is for wimps but a little lamb… now that's for tough guys, right? Who are you kidding?"

His words jolted her back to the present. He was right. What on earth had made her demonstrate this particular piece for him?

She met his eyes, letting him know his glare and belligerent tone couldn't push her away. She thought for a moment and then smiled. "You want something tough, big guy? How about sculpting a falcon?"

The boy's eyes widened. "What are you talking about?"

Almost before the words were out of his mouth, Sophie's fingers kneaded and shaped the clay.

"The falcon is a fast, powerful bird. Its eye is so precise, its power so awesome it can swoop down and capture other small birds in flight."

With one of her tools, she layered indentations resembling feathers in the extended wings and Jimmy watched in fascination.

"A falcon is a bird of prey. Far from a wimp." Sophie held up the small model and attached sharp, angled talons. "That's your last name, isn't it? Falcon?" When she'd finished, she held it out for Jimmy's inspection. "There are a million things you can create, Jimmy. With time, lessons and some effort on your part, you can let your imagination soar. Just like this falcon."

From the look of awe in his eyes, Sophie knew she'd captured his interest. The bad-guy persona disappeared and a vulnerable, hurt teenager stared at the molded shape in her hand and then back at her.

"Can you teach me to do that?"

"It's going to take much more than one class, Jimmy. It will demand a good deal of your time. I'll be happy to teach you…so will Mrs. Garrison…but it's all going to depend on you. How hard will you work? You have to be truly committed, not just for an hour here and there, if you plan on being an artist. You have to learn discipline and how to control your impulses when you face failures and rejections."

Emotions warred across his face. The tough guy. The child. Mistrust. Tentative hope. He glanced around the room, fidgeted in his seat and then looked back at the object in her hand.

"I can make anything? With clay, I mean?"

Sophie nodded. "Anything you can imagine and your fingers can shape. Are you willing to put in the time?"

Jimmy drew in a deep breath as though he needed extra strength to take the step he hoped might change his life, and nodded. "I want to make a falcon."

Sophie smiled. "Okay. Let's start with a block of brown clay."

"I appreciated your help today, Sophie," Martha said after the last of the teenagers had left and they were packing up their supplies. "You're great with the kids."

"I enjoyed it. It was fun. Reminded me of what it felt like when I used clay as an art medium for the first time."

"Cain tells me that you're quite a sculptor."

Sophie's cheeks heated. "I like working with clay. It relaxes me."

Martha nodded. "I wonder if you might be interested in helping out with the class on a regular basis."

"Me?" Sophie couldn't hide her look of surprise.

"I can't afford to pay much. But I think I can offer enough to make it worth your while two days a week. Also, I've applied for a grant. I'm hoping that in the near future I can expand the art classes into a daily program and work with the kids through the juvenile courts. If the grant is approved, it will allow me to offer you a full-time position with a more substantial salary."

Martha clasped Sophie's hand. "You're great with the kids. You have a treasure trove of experience to offer them. And I can really use the help. What do you say?"

Sophie couldn't believe it. Someone wanted to hire her… salary and everything…to teach something she'd been born and raised to do. Smiling so wide she thought her face would split, she said, "Thank you, Mrs. Garrison. I accept."

"Ohh, that's wonderful," Martha exclaimed. "Let me lock up and we'll stop by Holly's and celebrate."

Sophie excused herself and slipped out to the restroom. She'd just closed the door to a stall when she heard two women enter.

"I don't know what's gotten into Martha Garrison. Do you know who she had helping her with her art class today?"

"Elizabeth Weatherly's daughter."

"Exactly. I thought Martha's idea of running an art class for borderline delinquents was one of the most ridiculous ideas Pastor has ever supported. Now this! Everyone knows what happened to Elizabeth. She ran off with a wanted criminal. How could Martha have someone with her background around those teenagers?"

"Well, it makes perfect sense to me, Margaret. Birds of a feather and all that. Who would know how to relate to town trash better than trash?"

The blood drained from Sophie's face. Her eyes burned with unshed tears and her legs threatened to give out beneath her.

Trash? Was that what everyone thought of her?

The two women finished their business, washed their hands and left.

Sophie's heart pounded in her chest. How could she have been so stupid? To allow herself to think she might have finally found a home? Made some friends? Had a future here?

Her pain quickly changed to anger. She stepped into the hall and nearly barreled into Martha Garrison.

"What's the matter, dear? You're as pale as a ghost. Is everything all right?"

"Everything's fine. Look, I forgot I have some chores to do. I'm afraid I'll have to turn down celebrating at Holly's."

Sophie tried to slide past her but Martha reached out a hand and stopped her. "What happened?"

Sophie couldn't hold back her hurt and anger. "Two of the women in your church—two *Christian* women who are supposed to believe in Christ and act Christlike—reminded me of just who I am and where I fit in here."

Martha's expression registered shock. "Who said something to you? What did they say?"

Sophie sighed. "Nothing that isn't true." She gently released Martha's hand from her arm. "I appreciate your offer of employment, Mrs. Garrison. And I will accept it for now. But just until you find someone else to help you. After all, I'm still looking for my father. I don't know for sure how much longer I'm going to be in Promise, anyway."

"Sophie, tell me what happened."

"It doesn't matter. Really." She stepped around her. "I don't feel much like celebrating right now, that's all. Sorry."

"Where are you going?" Martha called after her.

"Home."

"But Holly is tied up at the diner until this evening and Cain doesn't want you out there by yourself."

"That's okay, Mrs. Garrison. I'm a big girl. Please tell

Holly not to come by this evening. I'm probably going to lock up and go to bed early anyway."

"Wait!" Mrs. Garrison's sharp tone made Sophie stop in her tracks and look back. "Come back to the house with me." She hurried to catch up with Sophie and then touched her arm. "Or let me come with you."

"I'll be fine, Mrs. Garrison. Don't worry."

She turned to go and Martha stopped her again, her voice softer this time. "I don't know what those women said to you. But I know from your reaction that it wasn't kind, and I'm sure it wasn't true."

Sophie dipped her head.

Martha Garrison gently patted her shoulder. "Belief in the Lord doesn't take away our sinful natures, honey. It's something we have to struggle with every day. Sometimes we aren't very successful. I'm so sorry that those women showed you their human side and not their Christian one."

Sophie knew the truth of those words in her heart but it didn't stop the hurt. Fresh tears burned her eyes. She nodded her head and hurried out of the hall before Mrs. Garrison could see her cry.

THIRTEEN

Cain flipped on the light switch. He eased out of his suit jacket and then settled into the leather chair behind his office desk. He halfheartedly leafed through the mail he'd carried inside. Nothing pressing. Except, of course, for the considerable-size check he'd received for payment on an insurance fraud case. It would be enough to meet this month's bills and allow him the extra time he needed to focus on Sophie's case.

He tossed the check in his top drawer. Getting up and crossing the room, he lifted a slat on the blinds and stared into the street. Not that there was much to see. Streetlamps. Occasional store lights. But it didn't matter if a full-size giraffe walked right past his window. He'd never notice. All he could see when he looked out his window anymore was Sophie—chasing oranges for Mrs. Gleason—stepping into the street—a black sedan barreling out of the alley.

He groaned. The last five days had been torture. Even though he knew Holly had stepped in and provided protection, even though his mother had made a point of visiting Sophie daily and even though he'd called her himself a half dozen times a day, it had been torture being away from her.

He missed seeing her impish, teasing smile. He missed the fiery spark of determination in her eyes. Who was he kidding? He missed everything about her more than he was willing to admit.

He'd thought it best for both of them if he distanced himself. Return things to a totally professional level and leave personal feelings out of it. He'd thought it would be easy not seeing her. He'd thought wrong.

He plopped back down in his chair. Fatigue settled into every bone of his body. He'd purposely pushed himself to squeeze two weeks' worth of work into five days, crisscrossing the state, taking on and finishing jobs he could have easily assigned to others. Pushing himself to endure a schedule he'd never have asked or expected from anyone else.

Punishing himself.

Because he'd told Sophie the truth about the end of his career, about the thread of life he'd held on to for the longest time…about Lucy. He'd finally revealed to another human being the toll it had taken on him, not just physically but emotionally. It had been a huge weight lifted from his shoulders. Acknowledging the mistakes and the consequences of his actions helped him begin to deal with the feelings he'd buried for years. But the relief dissipated when he realized he'd done it again. He'd allowed himself to become emotionally involved with someone on a case, and it scared him to death.

So he ran.

He buried himself in work. He'd tried to convince himself he could turn back the clock and return to a strictly professional relationship. He could forget the sound of her laughter, the scent of her skin, the touch of her lips.

He'd been as successful at that as he had been at forgetting how to breathe.

He closed his eyes and leaned his head against the back of his chair.

So, what now, Lord? Where did I go from here? Have I

wandered off the path You intended for my life? Or did You plant Sophie on that path? Is it Your intention that I give her my heart or is it my own human weakness drawing me to her?

He wiped a hand over his face and slumped forward, his elbows on his desk.

She's lost her faith, Lord. She doesn't believe You answer our prayers. How do I make her understand? You answer every prayer. Sometimes Your answer is 'yes'. Sometimes it's 'not yet, wait'. And sometimes Your answer is 'no'. But You answer. Speak to my heart, Lord. What am I supposed to do?

The office door opened and two men, dressed in dark suits on this warm summer night, stepped into the room.

Cain sat up straight. He knew instantly who they were. Trouble with a capital *T.*

"Good evening, gentlemen. What can I do for you?"

They approached the desk. The taller, leaner man held out his hand, flashing a badge.

"Federal marshals, Mr. Garrison. It's time we have a talk."

Sophie carried a cup of freshly brewed iced tea and a book from her massive to-be-read pile and settled comfortably into her favorite chair. Silence surrounded her in the empty cottage and she smiled. She'd loved that Cain and his family had gone out of their way to fill her every waking moment with their presence. It had been reassuring. She'd felt protected.

But, at times, Sophie had also felt overwhelmed, out of her element. She'd grown up a homeschooled only child with a father who worked long into the evenings on his craft. She'd learned to enjoy her solitude, even thrived in it. Of course, if the solitude lasted too long, if her father locked himself away for hours, sometimes days, working on a new project, she admitted to being lonely. But after two weeks of someone nearby at all times she craved her personal space, this delicious time to herself to do anything, or nothing, as she saw fit.

She knew she'd be safe. She'd barely taken her eyes off the rearview mirror the entire drive from town and confirmed she hadn't been followed. Every window in the house was locked. Both the front and back doors had multiple dead bolt locks. Professional strength pepper spray rested in the right pocket of her jeans and her cell phone with 911 on speed dial sat on the table beside her chair.

Yep, she was safe. She could take care of herself. Wouldn't her dad be proud of her?

Tucking her legs beneath her she turned to the first page of her book and entered a world of suspense, intrigue and romance—a safe world where she didn't have to be the heroine in her own melodrama.

Afternoon shadows melted into darkness. Sophie turned on several lamps, made herself a sandwich, took a glance outside to reassure herself that the black sedan hadn't made a stealth reappearance, and returned with delight to her novel.

An hour later she finished the last page and closed the book with satisfaction. Pins and needles in her left leg from sitting on it too long caused her to limp in circles as she tried to work the circulation back into her leg. As she circled the chair for a third time, a sound caught and held her attention.

A car was moving up the graveled drive.

Sophie's eyes flew to the clock. It was after nine.

Holly.

The diner closed at eight. She wished she had respected Sophie's request not to come. She should be home tonight sleeping in her own bed instead of aiming for Sophie's sofa. She didn't need protection tonight. She was doing fine on her own.

She got up from the chair and hurried to the door. Maybe she shouldn't let her in. Maybe she should just assure Holly that she was fine and insist on her going home tonight. But did friends treat friends that way? She'd never had a best friend before and she didn't want to hurt her feelings.

She peered out the side window. Even though she couldn't get a good look at the car in the dark, she knew from its shape that it wasn't Holly's fire-red convertible. This car was in the shadows too much to identify the make and model. Slowly, it rolled up in front of the cottage and stopped. Once the headlights were turned off, the moon was the only outside illumination.

All Sophie could see was the dark figure of a man exiting the driver's side door. Her fingers clasped the pepper spray. When she realized she'd left her cell phone behind, she raced back, retrieved it and held it tightly in her left hand, her thumb ready to press speed dial. She approached the door and drew the curtain back. Her breath caught in her throat.

Cain.

Her heart leapt but this time in anticipation, not fear. Her eyes drank him in as if he were the perfect ice-cold drink on a hot summer day. She noticed the slump of his shoulders, his limp more pronounced. He was exhausted. And yet he had still taken the time to come and see her.

Sophie's fingers flew over the locks and flung open the door. She'd wanted to say something profound, something witty, something that would make him happy that he'd come to see her no matter how exhausted he was.

Instead, she said, "Hi."

"Hi, yourself." He lowered the hand he'd raised to knock on the door and grinned at her. "Tell me you knew one hundred percent it was me before you opened that door."

How could he not know that she'd recognize him any-where? Her heart skipped each time he was near. Her pulse raced and her lips took on a mind of their own with a continuous grin. If she were blind, her heart would recognize him. There was a crackling in the air between them. A heightened awareness of his scent, the feel of his touch, right down to the gently calloused tips of his fingers.

The past five days had seemed like five years. She wanted to throw her arms around his neck and tell him how much she missed him and how happy she was to see him again.

Instead, she held up the pepper spray and cell phone. "I was prepared for battle on the remote chance it wasn't you."

He grinned and inclined his head toward the living room. "Mind if I come in?"

She opened the door wider.

"I hope you don't mind if I make myself comfortable. It's been a long day." Removing his tie, he tucked it into a side pocket, slipped off his suit jacket and placed it on the arm of the sofa. He plopped down and stretched his long legs in front of him. Almost absently he massaged his thigh and Sophie knew he was more than exhausted. He was in pain.

"Can I get you anything?"

He eyed the partial remains of her sandwich. "If it's not too much trouble, one of those would be great. I haven't eaten since breakfast in the airport this morning."

"No problem. While I'm at it, how about something for the pain in your leg?"

His eyes flew to her. He seemed surprised at her perceptiveness and nodded.

Sophie returned a few minutes later and handed him a platter, including two pills to ease his leg pain, and then sat in the chair opposite him.

He swallowed the pills, then attacked the sandwich as if it were a succulent filet mignon instead of a ham and Swiss cheese on rye with side helpings of pickles and potato chips.

She waited for him to finish before she smiled and asked, "So, stranger, where have you been?"

Those few words changed the atmosphere in the room instantly from comfortable and friendly to tense and awkward in the time it would take to flip a light switch.

"I've called you every day. I had to take care of business."

The defensiveness in his tone didn't surprise her. People running away usually put up a defensive shield. Sophie's heart hammered in her chest. Should she ignore the elephant in the room or force the issue that stood between them?

The shy, scared Sophie she used to be would have backed off. Truthfully, that Sophie wouldn't have had the guts to flirt or ask personal questions in the first place. The new, improved Sophie knew that in this world a person needs to know how to be self-reliant—and sometimes bold. Circumstances had forced her to grow up quite a bit in the past month. She'd found an inner strength she hadn't realized she possessed. She understood now that she was able to stand on her own two feet and she could think for herself.

And right now all she could think about was shooting the elephant in the room, so they could clear the air between them, so she would know where they stood with each other.

"You were great about calling every day. And I really appreciate the extra attention from Holly and your mom." She smiled, keeping her tone soft and soothing.

He nodded and took a sip of his iced tea.

"But I need to know, Cain." She caught and held his gaze. "What made you run away? Talking about Lucy? Or kissing me?"

A thundercloud washed across his expression. "I didn't run away." He spat the words out in a clipped, don't-mess-with-me-I'm-too-tired tone.

"Sure you did." Her right toe tapped her nervous energy

against the carpet. "I'm getting to be an expert on the subject of running away. My dad…myself…you."

He stared at her but didn't answer.

Her tone softened to a whisper. "I missed you, Cain."

The tension in the room was as palpable as if a third party were present.

Slowly, she crossed over and sat down beside him. "Please, Cain. I need to understand. Was it the kiss? Or our conversation about Lucy? Did I push too hard?"

Push too hard? She actually had no idea what a gift it had been for him to be able to share his buried pain with another human being, to be able to release some of that pent-up hurt.

He gently cupped the side of her face. "Sophie…you're right. You did push." He struggled with putting his emotions into words. He brushed an errant strand of hair behind her ear. "And I did run."

He clasped her hand, keeping her close so she wouldn't move away. It took him a moment to realize she wasn't planning to go anywhere. Her sea-green eyes moved over him with tenderness, understanding. The soft smile pulling at her rosy lips encouraged him.

He leaned his head back on the sofa, closed his eyes and ran his other hand through his hair. "This isn't the conversation I'd planned to have when I drove out here tonight, Sophie." He felt her body stiffen at his words.

"Why did you come?"

He opened his eyes. One look at the questions…the subtle fear in her eyes…broke his heart.

"Has there been a break in the case? Something I should know?"

He released her hand and slid his arm around her shoulders. "Federal marshals came to see me tonight. What I have to say isn't going to be easy for you to hear."

FOURTEEN

"Federal marshals?" Sophie's hand flew to her chest. She jumped to her feet and faced him. "Did they find my father? Has he been arrested? Is he…is he dead?"

"Sorry. I don't know anything more about your father's disappearance."

"The feds don't know where my father is?"

Cain shook his head.

"Then why did they come?"

"They showed up in my office to question me. Apparently, Big Brother has any computer searches of your father's real name flagged and it brought them running."

"Wait a minute." Sophie started pacing back and forth. "They came to you because *they* are looking for my dad? And they thought you might know where he is?"

"They wanted to know why I was investigating your dad. They wanted to know who I was working for."

She froze in place and had to force out her words. "Me? They wanted to know about me?"

"Yes."

"And what did you tell them."

"I told them my client list was confidential and I refused to comment unless they brought a court order."

Sophie blinked hard. Her legs trembled and she sat down

on the wooden coffee table in front of the sofa before she fell. Her knees brushed against Cain's. He leaned forward and clasped her hands in his. The warmth of his skin, the strength of his grasp calmed her, made her feel safe.

"Why, Cain? Are the stories about him true? Is my father on the run from the law?"

"Not exactly."

Sophie thought her head would explode. What was going on? Why was Cain being so cryptic?

"Here." Cain handed her his iced tea.

"I don't need your iced tea, Cain. I need answers. What's going on?"

Cain sighed heavily. He sat back on the sofa, pulling her off the coffee table so she could sit beside him. "I'm torn, Sophie. I have information you need to know but…"

"But what? You think it will hurt me? You think I'm some fragile little flower that can't handle bad news?" She glared at him. "For your information, Mr. Garrison, I've been hit with both barrels over and over again for the past month and I'm still standing, so no more dancing around. I've paid you to find out information about my father. So deliver that information…. Now."

Cain couldn't help himself and laughed out loud. It took him a second to compose himself and then, still grinning, he said, "Wow, I wasn't expecting that reaction. And you're right. You've been a pillar of strength through all of this. I firmly believe, Miss Sophia Joy Clarkston Gimmelli, that you can handle just about anything. You have a backbone made of steel. It's one of the things I admire about you the most."

He pulled her to her feet. "Let's go out on the porch. It's a nice night. We can sit on the swing. I promise no more stalling. I'll tell you everything." He crossed his heart and smiled encouragingly.

He slid his arm around her shoulders and pulled her close.

Sophie liked the way she fit comfortably against his side, almost like jigsaw puzzle pieces meshed perfectly together. She just hoped before this night was over she'd find a way to make him see how well they fit together, too.

"Fine. Let me grab a pitcher of iced tea and some glasses. I'll be right out."

Once outside, she poured their drinks and handed one to Cain. She lit some citronella candles she used both for light and bug repellent before settling down beside him on the porch swing.

He threw his arm over her shoulder and cradled her against his side. The faint scent of his aftershave teased her nostrils and tempted her to burrow closer. The light summer breeze, a welcome relief from the prior heat of the day, tossed an errant strand of hair across her face. She reached up and tucked the hair behind her ear.

Cain rocked the swing in a slow rhythmic movement with his foot. The sound of crickets, frogs and small nocturnal animals rustling through the brush serenaded them.

Sophie thought this moment was perfect. Perfect weather. Perfect location. Perfect guy. A dream come true. And she didn't want it to come to a crashing end. So she remained silent, resting her head in the crook of his arm, relishing his nearness and simply enjoying the moment.

But like all moments, perfect or not, time passes and Cain broke the silence.

"The marshals tried to play hardball at first. Shooting a million questions at me and answering none. But we continued to talk. Eventually, they thought it would be in their best interest if they shared what they knew and then see where it would get them, since nothing they were about to tell me would jeopardize their current investigation."

Sophie nodded and took another sip of her tea.

"Sophie, you already know that your father was the son

of Vincent Gimmelli. The feds helped fill in the gaps to the past."

"This is the part I'm not going to like, isn't it?"

"Probably. But it's a part you need to know."

She nodded. "Go ahead, I'm all ears."

"Your father was not just the son of one of the capos of organized crime. As you already know, he was the *only* son and heir to everything." He let that sink in and took a sip of tea before continuing. "He should have been groomed to be his father's replacement as head of the 'family.' But Vincent didn't want his son to follow in his footsteps."

Sophie tried to stop her teeth from chattering as she listened to this story of her family history. "You're telling me that even though my grandfather ran the whole thing, was king of the hill, so to speak, that he didn't want my dad as his heir to the throne? Why?"

This time it was Cain's turn to lift a questioning eyebrow.

Sophie stood up and began to pace back and forth on the porch. She wondered why Cain was grinning at her until she realized she was kneading a block of clay in her hand as she paced.

"Your grandfather had a love for the arts. Rumor has it that as a very young child he displayed quite a creative side of his own. Won a few art awards in grammar school."

Cain rested a foot on his knee and leaned back in the swing. "He'd been denied the opportunity to follow that dream…to build that talent. When Vincent recognized your father's talent at an early age, he decided to live vicariously through him and shielded him from his business.

"Of course, as your father matured into an intelligent young man, Vinnie wasn't able to hide his business dealings from him as easily. The feds told me when their surveillance team discovered how upset and angry Dominic was with his father, they thought he'd be an easy mark for them to turn him into a state's witness.

"Before they could make a move, Vinnie shipped your dad off to school in Europe. He went to college, got a master's degree in art, lived in Paris, England, Italy. When your father finally moved back to the States, your dad refused to return to Maryland. That's why he accepted a teaching job in Virginia. And that's where he met your mother. She'd signed up for a summer art class. He was the instructor."

Sophie stopped her pacing and leaned against the porch railing and stared out into the darkness.

She felt Cain's presence behind her, felt his breath fan the back of her neck.

"You okay, Soph?"

She nodded but didn't turn to face him. "It's all sort of sad in a way. My dad was a good guy. It must have been so difficult for him when he learned the truth about his father, to have to sever ties with a man I'm sure my dad loved. And then to have to live his life being unjustly accused of things because of who his family was."

She glanced back and smiled at him. "But at least he met my mother. And fell in love with her. That had to bring him happiness." She sighed. "But he found himself accused again…and forced to run. My parents obviously loved one another deeply."

"More than you know."

Sophie turned to face him. The graveness in his expression made her pause. "What?" She tilted her head and stared at him when he didn't immediately answer her. "What else do you know, Cain?"

"Your mother was so young, Sophie…naive…idealistic… sort of a Pollyanna. She told your father that the only way she would leave Promise with him was if he went to the authorities and told them what he knew."

Sophie gasped. "She asked him to betray his own father?"

Cain sighed. "She asked him to do the right thing, to make the world a safer place, to protect the people being exploited by his father's business."

"Wow," Sophie kneaded the clay faster. "Obviously, he did as she requested. She left with him."

"He told her he would. That's why she went with him. But when it came down to the wire, he couldn't do it."

"What do you mean?" Sophie was glad the candlelight wasn't strong enough to reveal the mixed emotions racing across her face.

"He loved your mother…but he also loved his father, even if he didn't approve of the things he did. When the feds first approached him, he turned them down."

"Wow, my mom must have felt betrayed. Why didn't she leave him?"

"I imagine she stayed because she loved him. And she understood the deep relationship between father and son. It's one thing to be angry with a parent, to not approve of their actions, to close yourself off from them. It's quite another to be the one responsible for putting that parent behind bars for the rest of his life. I think your dad kept convincing your mother that he would do the right thing he just needed time to work up the courage. But time slipped away and his promises became nothing more than empty words."

"So what happened?"

"You did. The feds got wind about an internal battle in Vincent Gimmelli's ranks. Some people thought it was time for him to retire, permanently. The feds approached your dad. They told him that the people trying to overthrow Vinnie might decide to use your dad and his family as pawns against him. The feds told your dad their sources had confirmed this and that he and your mother were in danger. With you on the way, Dominic felt he had no choice. He agreed to testify against his father and enter the witness protection program."

"I don't understand. My dad and I were never in the witness protection program. I know I missed a lot of things growing up, but I don't believe I'd have missed feds appearing in our lives on a regular basis checking up on us."

Cain's eyes darkened and his mouth pulled into a tight, straight line.

"What haven't you told me?" She noted his hesitation and placed a hand gently on his cheek. "Tell me," she whispered. "I need to know it all."

"Your parents did go into the program. But before your father could testify, your mother was killed." He removed her hand, kissed the back of it and stared into her eyes. "You were told she had been killed in an auto accident."

"Yes?" Her chest tightened and she could hardly breathe as she braced herself for what he was about to say.

"It wasn't an accident, Sophie. She was killed in a car bomb."

She blinked…tried to breathe…blinked again.

"Your parents, living under their new identities, were leaving an art exhibit. When they reached their car, your mother had forgotten something. She asked your father to retrieve it for her and said she'd pull the car up front and wait for him. When she turned the key in the ignition, the car exploded. Your father was close enough to be knocked to the ground with a serious concussion, but that didn't stop him. The burns on his hands came from trying to pull your mother out of the car."

Tears streamed down Sophie's face. She remembered questioning her father about the terrible scars on his hands and arms. He made up a story about being injured experimenting with chemicals during an art project.

A car bomb? The pain in Sophie's chest was almost too much to bear.

Cain brushed the tears from her cheek with his thumb. "I'm so sorry."

"What happened then?"

Cain led her back to the swing and gently rocked it as if the rhythm would help soothe her. "Your dad knew then that witness protection couldn't protect him…or you. And he believed he'd have a better chance protecting you on his own."

"I don't understand. If his father found him the first time, what made my dad think they wouldn't find us again?"

"I don't know, Sophie. Maybe someday we can ask him."

His words caught her attention. "You think he might still be alive?"

"I don't know. The feds think he's dead. They believe that when the Mob caught up with him, they killed him. But they also don't think they found the evidence your father had against them. They think your father left the evidence with you as leverage for protection. That's why the feds believe the Mob is looking for you. The feds want to offer you their protection in exchange for that evidence."

Sophie let the information sink in before speaking. She almost laughed out loud but realized Cain would think her insane. She already believed she was caught in a living nightmare…. Now this.

The Mob was targeting her for information she didn't have. They must be the ones responsible for her near hit-and-run, her ransacked home, nearly being run off the road at the cemetery. Suddenly, the dark, evil eyes of the driver following her earlier today popped into her mind and her stomach roiled.

Federal marshals wanted her, too, for their witness protection program. Wanted to take her away from Promise, from

Holly and Mrs. Garrison, from Cain. For the first time since this nightmare had begun she was grateful she didn't have the evidence to give them.

Sophie stood up. She clasped her arms tightly around her body. "Well, it's all over now, isn't it? The feds are convinced my father is dead. And we both know I don't have any evidence to hand over to them or to the Mob. So it's over."

Cain stood and faced her. "Over? Nothing's over. What are you talking about?"

"You've solved the case. I don't need your services anymore."

"Are you out of your mind? The Mob is after you. You've never needed my protection more."

He thinks I need his protection.

Not his love. Not him.

Sophie smiled and hoped the sadness that permeated her being wouldn't show in her face. "Your job is done, Cain. You're a detective, not a bodyguard. You found the information I asked you to find. Send me the bill."

He recoiled as if she'd struck him. It took all the strength in her body to stand there and stare back into his angry, confused eyes.

That's right, Cain. I'm not your client anymore. Maybe now you can admit your feelings for me without feeling guilty for crossing a professional line...without fearing I'll hurt you like she did.

"Sophie." He clasped her forearms. "You are the most infuriating, stubborn woman I have ever met."

"What happened to 'Sophie, you have a backbone of steel'?" She grinned.

He looked like he wanted to shake her. "Stop fooling around. This case is far from over and I'm not going anywhere. Someone has killed your father and now they are trying to kill you. Do you get that?"

"Of course, I get that. I'm not stupid, Cain. Or foolish. I know it's a probability the Mob has killed my father. But there's another scenario, too."

"Really? And what's that?"

"My father isn't dead. He's hiding. He's running for his life. And there's no way I'm going to have any part in leading anyone to him. I don't want to know where he is anymore so no one can force me to do or say anything that could harm him. I don't want to know where…or even if…he hid evidence."

She stepped closer. Her fingers ever so gently traced the stubble on his face. She gazed into his troubled, exhausted eyes. "It's over, Cain. As of this minute, I'm not your client anymore. Go home. Get some rest."

"But you're not safe…."

She held up the pepper spray. "I'm as safe as I'm going to be. You can't be my bodyguard twenty-four hours a day. I hired you to locate my father."

"But I didn't."

She smiled into his eyes. "You did more, Cain. You gave me back my life. You found out who I really am. Where I come from. Where I belong. It's enough." She pressed her lips lightly against his and smiled. "It's everything."

"I don't like this," he growled like a wounded bear.

Sophie laughed. "You don't have to like it." She gently pushed him toward the top step of the porch. "But you have to go. Get some sleep. It will seem clearer to you in the morning."

He took a step away and then stopped.

"Before I leave, I want you to know that I'm not mad that you pushed me to confide in you about Lucy."

"You're not?" Doubt rang in her voice.

He stared into her eyes. "I'm grateful. It's the first time I shared that information with anyone. All that pain and hurt and guilt was bottled up inside of me, festering, growing. And you helped me get it out."

She smiled but remained quiet. Waiting. Letting him tell things in his own time, in his own way.

"I'm not saying it was a magic cure for me. I still have strong emotions I have to deal with regarding that time in my life." He kissed her forehead. "But because of you, now I have a real shot at doing exactly that."

"Cain, you can talk to me anytime, about anything."

He brushed his fingers down her cheek and hugged her a little closer. "I know that, Soph. You're a good friend."

Friend?

The blood drained from her face and an unsettling feeling twisted her stomach.

"That's why I threw myself into my work. My emotions were spilling all over the place. I'm not used to feeling that way and I needed the space to clear my head."

"And did you?" she asked. "Clear your head?"

"I realized I was on the verge of making a horrible mistake. I was letting myself plunge headlong into another personal relationship with someone involved in a case I was working."

Mistake? Her stomach clenched. This conversation was not going the way she'd hoped at all.

"Everything was happening so fast I needed to take a step back. I needed to assure myself I wasn't doing the same stupid thing again."

Sophie stepped away, hating the slight distance she put between them, already missing the warmth of his body as she broke their contact.

"And what great discovery did you make, Cain?" She surprised herself with how calm her voice sounded. Her insides were tumbling every which way they could but at least her voice wasn't letting her down.

"No mistake, Sophie. I've realized you're becoming one of my best friends. How can that be wrong?"

Her hopes tumbled to her feet. She looked into his stupid, grinning face and wanted to hit him.

"Friends?"

"Always and forever. I hope you feel the same way about me."

She smiled weakly in return. "Believe me, Cain. You can't imagine how I feel about you."

"Good. Then you agree. We can be friends and still keep this situation between us professional."

"Sure. Professional." Tears burned at the back of her eyes but she'd die before she'd shed one in front of him. So he was giving her the brush-off. Because of Lucy. She suddenly understood why people swore.

Is it really that easy for you, Cain? To kiss me? To hold me? And try to convince yourself that nothing remarkable, nothing special is blossoming between us?

And then a lightbulb went on inside her mind and she smiled. He was still running. He *did* feel something special for her and it frightened him. Okay. She understood. After the horrible betrayal from Lucy, it was normal for him to be gun-shy. She'd just have to find a way to convince him he could trust his feelings again. That she wasn't Lucy. She wouldn't betray him…ever.

A peace settled over her. All was not lost. There'd be time for him to come to his senses. And firing him from the case was exactly what she needed to do if she wanted to release him from that "professional" wall he'd erected between them.

"I'm sorry I had nothing but bad news for you today." Then he kissed her, gently, softly, almost as if he were trying to heal the aching hurt he knew she held inside.

"Leave, Cain." She pushed lightly against his chest. "Go home and get some sleep."

"I'll leave…but not until I'm sure you're safely inside."

She started to speak and his fingers silenced her lips.

"A lot has been said here tonight. We both need to get some sleep. Clear our heads. We'll talk again tomorrow."

He led her inside. She stood in the doorway and promised to lock the door as soon as he made it to the car. Before he left, he turned on the top step and looked at her long and hard as if he was being compelled to say something more.

"Sophie, my mother called and told me what happened at the church today. I'm so sorry you had to go through that."

She shrugged. "It's over and done with."

"Maybe so," he said. "But I want you to remember when you think about everything that happened today, and you will—even though I'm hoping you'll be able to get a good night's sleep and not dwell on things—I want you to understand something really important."

"What's that?"

He stared at her long and hard. "People disappoint people. They do it all the time. I don't want to ever disappoint you—I hope I never do—but if I do…" He shrugged his shoulders and gave her that lopsided grin of his. "Knowing me, I probably already have." His expression sobered and his eyes darkened. "But God never will, Soph. If you can count on anything, you can count on that."

FIFTEEN

Sophie pulled back the curtain and shaded her eyes against the bright morning sun. She'd slept poorly, tossing and turning most of the night, jumping at every creak and imagined sound she heard. So much for being the big, brave I-can-stand-on-my-own-and-don't-need-anyone girl she professed to be.

As hard as she'd tried last night to rest her body, it had been impossible to rest her mind. She spent most of the night second-guessing her decisions. Should she have told Holly about receiving the threatening telephone call? Should she have told Sheriff Dalton about the black sedan following her yesterday even though she had no proof it really had been? And most of all, should she have told Cain? He'd left last night believing there'd been no further threatening incidents for over a week. She hadn't lied to him. He just hadn't asked her the right questions.

Sins of omission. Hmm.

Besides, he had to leave. She'd fired him.

The beginning of a smile twisted the corner of her mouth as she remembered the shocked expression on his face. She only hoped when he'd rested and had some time to think about things that he'd realize what she'd really done—opened the door to the possibility of more between them.

She took a morning shower, a cold one, and hoped the

frigid temperature would shock her system awake. Toweling herself dry, she dressed in a red tank top, denim shorts and sandals. She pulled her hair back and fastened it in a bun on top of her head so she wouldn't have it hanging on her neck in the heat.

This is just another day. Relax. Worrying never gets a person anywhere.

As she finished her breakfast and cleaned up the kitchen, she allowed herself to think about the devastating news Cain had delivered last night. Were the federal marshals right? Had someone killed her father? A wave of pain seized her heart at the thought she might never see him again.

Or was he on the run? Frightened. Hiding. Alone.

Although she still wished he'd confided in her, she understood now why he'd left without a word. He'd been trying to protect her—just as he'd done his entire life.

Sophie pushed back the curtain over the kitchen sink. Her eyes carefully skimmed the woods for any sign of danger and found none. No shadows. No people hiding in the brush. No obvious threats. But she knew someone was out there. She could feel it. She'd felt it every day she'd been in Promise. Someone was watching every move she made—or else she'd watched too many movies and was making herself paranoid.

Paranoid or not, she chose to be vigilant and err on the side of caution.

After all these years on the run, how had the Mob found them? And why now? Would a crime family actually search over twenty-two years for someone? That joke about the only way to retire from the Mob was six feet under wasn't really a joke, was it?

She placed her dishes in the rack to dry and emptied the sink.

And now these evil men were following her. The memory

of the man's black, lifeless eyes in her rearview mirror flashed through her mind and chills slithered over her spine.

Maybe she should have told Cain about the whispered phone threat and the black sedan following her.

No. Bad move. Can't do that.

She needed him to come back on his own…because he wanted to…because he needed to…because he needed her. Sophie touched her lips with the tip of her fingers. Their kiss had been meaningful, something special definitely blossoming between them. And she knew he'd felt it, too. He'd call. She just had to be patient and wait.

Yeah, right. Patient. Then why hadn't she been able to take her eyes off the phone the entire time she'd spent eating her cereal and finishing her second cup of coffee?

She wasn't his client anymore. No professional conflicts. Freedom to explore their budding relationship further. Freedom to find out if what they had could lead to something more…something serious and lasting.

He'd call.

She checked her cell phone for messages.

None.

She crossed the room and picked up the receiver to check for a dial tone.

The familiar buzz sounded in her ear. Phone's working. That's good. He's going to call. Just not yet.

She left the kitchen, walked over and looked out the front door. Again, she did a quick surveillance of her property and the surrounding woods. Everything A-OK.

What should she do now? Ever since the whispered demand to give back what was theirs, she'd ransacked every nook and cranny of this home and tried to find the "evidence" that everyone thought she possessed but had come up empty-handed.

They were out there. She could feel them watching her.

Waiting. Hoping she'd lead them right to her father. She couldn't allow that to happen. But she wasn't sure how to avoid it.

Should she stay in Promise and hope her father stayed far away? Or would he make his way back here to see that she was okay? That was what the Mob wanted him to do. And knowing how much her father loved her, deep in her gut she was terrified that that's exactly what he'd do…if he could.

So did she have to leave Promise?

Her eyes burned with tears. How could she? This was home now. She had a job with Mrs. Garrison teaching art to teens. She had a best friend for the first time in her life with Holly. And she had Cain…something special, something wonderful was happening between them…even if he didn't realize it yet.

But if leaving meant keeping her father safe…

Oh, Lord, help me make the right decision.

The prayer entered her mind with lightning speed, as if talking to God was natural and normal. Sophie felt a wave of relief. It *was* natural for her to talk to God. He'd been there with her through every waking moment of her life. And He was with her now, even though she had turned away. In the quiet of this cottage, in the sunlit glow of the morning, she felt His presence—still. A lone tear slid down her face. She dropped to her knees and prayed.

God, please forgive me. I've been acting like a spoiled child, throwing temper tantrums because I didn't like the circumstances of my life, because answers didn't come when I wanted them. But You have Your own plans for my life. You have guided me and loved me all my life. I beg You to forgive me and guide me now. I am so sorry, Lord. I don't know what to do. I don't know where to turn.

When she lifted her eyes, she spotted the Bible she'd carelessly tossed on the end table when she'd first arrived in Promise—her mother's Bible. She picked it up and caressed the soft leather. Sophie sat down, gently opened the well-worn pages and began to read.

When she came to Matthew 10:26–28, "But don't be afraid of those who threaten you. For the time is coming when the truth will be revealed: their secret plots will become public information," Sophie smiled. A feeling of warmth and comfort filled every inch of her spirit. Sophie knew God had forgiven her. She'd come home.

Cain groaned, glanced bleary-eyed at his watch and groaned again. He pulled himself out of bed and reached for his Bible. Almost noon. He'd never slept this long before. Then again, he didn't know if falling on the bed fully dressed and passing out in an almost comatose state counted as sleep. But he'd needed it. It had been the first full night's sleep he'd had in weeks.

He opened his Bible and began his morning prayers. When he was finished he went into the bathroom. He looked in the mirror, ran his hand over the thick stubble on his face and reached for his razor. He looked like he'd had a bad night out on the town. The reality was he'd had five bad nights—trying to run away from his feelings for Sophie.

She'd fired him!

He dabbed shaving cream on his face and grinned at his reflection. Imagine that, firing him. That girl had a backbone of steel and he loved that about her. He loved her resiliency, her optimism, her faith.

He knew deep down she hadn't lost her faith. All of her actions spoke otherwise. She'd never have come to church with his family, would never have agreed to teach a craft class with his mother for the sole purpose of introducing the kids to the Lord if she didn't have faith.

No. She'd been hurt and angry and definitely afraid. She'd find her way back—and he'd help her. Now that she'd fired him.

His grin widened. He'd been too tired last night to see the bigger picture, to realize what she was doing, and had left defeated, confused and exhausted. But a good night's sleep and his morning talk with the Lord had put everything into perspective. Sophie, his black-haired, green-eyed spit-fire knew that he'd never allow himself to pursue her if she remained his client—so she'd fired him.

He laughed out loud. Lord, he loved that girl. Then he sobered when the truth of those words hit him. They'd only known each other for a couple of weeks. But they had an entire lifetime to get to know one another. Cain trusted the Lord to guide his path, and there was no question in his mind anymore that the Lord intended that path to include Sophie.

He dressed quickly and downed a quick cup of coffee before heading out the door. He might not be officially on the case anymore but Sophie still needed his help. Somehow he had to discover the truth. Were the feds right? Was Sophie's father dead? Or was Sophie right? Her father was still alive and Sophie might be the bait leading the killers straight to him. Cain didn't know how he was going to find out, but he knew he wouldn't leave her side until they had some answers, no matter how long it took.

He laced up his running shoes and locked the front door. He tapped his fingers against his thigh. No pain today. Wonderful what a couple of pills and a good night's sleep could do. He headed for his car. He wondered if Sophie liked to jog…slowly, of course.

* * *

Sophie stood up and stretched her legs and then her back. She'd been weeding the front flower beds for hours and the outside of the cottage beamed under her tender loving care. Wildflowers danced along the porch foundation. Rhododendron bushes graced each corner of the house like beautiful sentinels standing guard. And the rosebushes bordering the brick walkway leading from the dirt drive to the house filled the air with a fragrance she didn't find in store-bought flowers anymore.

She cupped her hand over her eyes and looked up. The sun's height and the intensity of the heat told her she had worked well into the afternoon.

Still no call from Cain.

Okay. He needed more time to think things over. She could live with that. But she certainly wasn't going to sit by the phone anymore and wait. That was stupid and clingy—both adjectives she never wanted connected to her name.

She glanced around her garden and smiled. She knew what she was going to do. She leaned down and picked a bouquet of wildflowers. And she knew just who she wanted to give them to.

Less than fifteen minutes later, Sophie eased her car into the cemetery. She'd always liked coming here with her father. Not that she was crazy over cemeteries. Obviously, she wished she could be visiting her mother in person. But when Sophie and her father had made their annual visits to her mother's grave, it meant that, for at least a couple of days, they were home—in Promise—the only place she'd ever felt she had some roots.

But now she might have to leave again…permanently.

Instead of lingering on that unwanted possibility, she glanced at the beautiful bouquet of wildflowers on the seat beside her, picked them up and slid out of the car. She had never met her mother, but she'd bet if she had that her mom would have loved wildflowers, too. Especially ones grown in front of her childhood cottage.

She walked the short path to the top of the rise, humming under her breath. She approached the grave resting beneath the large oak tree and gasped. The bouquet fell from her fingers and flowers splayed across her feet.

On her mother's grave, in front of the headstone, stood another headstone made of cardboard. In crude black letters, someone had written: Sophia Joy Gimmelli...Time's Up...R.I.P.

SIXTEEN

Sophie's mind exploded with questions. How could this be happening? Who could have done this? Her eyes darted in every direction looking for someone, anyone. She was alone. Alone in a cemetery, staring at a homemade headstone with her name on it.

Oh, God, what do I do?

A small voice inside her head commanded her to get help. Without a second's hesitation, she turned and raced back to the car. It wasn't until she was safely inside, the car doors locked, the engine idling, that she dared to breathe.

Her hands trembled as she clasped the steering wheel. She tried to quiet her mind, calm her senses. If someone was trying to kill her, they probably would have done it by now. For the past twenty-four hours, she'd been alone and accessible for the first time in weeks. No, whoever it was wanted to frighten her. And they had done a really good job.

She needed to get to Cain. She needed to tell him everything—the telephone call demanding evidence everyone believed she possessed but she hadn't been able to find, the black sedan riding her bumper all the way into town yesterday, and now this.

Time's Up. R.I.P.

A cold, deathly shiver crawled up her spine.

She closed her eyes and forced herself to focus her thoughts on the problem at hand. She was alone and, for the moment, safe. She wasn't going to be killed by a resident of the cemetery.

When the initial shock started to wear off, she was able to think rationally. This wasn't a problem she needed to take to Cain. She needed to do just the opposite. She needed to prove to him, and to herself, that she really was self-sufficient, intelligent and able to make her own decisions.

It was time to call Sheriff Dalton and tell *him* everything. Even if she couldn't prove that she'd received a threatening call or that a car had tailgated her, she had tangible evidence with the handmade headstone that someone was targeting her. He wouldn't be able to dismiss her as delusional or, worse, having criminal intentions of her own.

Satisfied with her decision, she took one more glance around the grounds. Still no one. Her eyes returned to the top of the rise for one more fleeting glance at her mother's grave. Someone had been here intent on scaring her—or worse. When were they going to understand she didn't have what they wanted? How much longer was this torture going to continue? Would she ever be able to visit her mother's grave again and not have the image of her own tombstone indelibly burned into her brain?

Slipping the transmission into drive, she eased her car through the cemetery gates. Once she had a plan, her fear subsided, her trembling ceased and she could breathe normally again. Pulling her cell phone from her purse, she pressed the speed dial number she'd programmed into her phone for the sheriff. Sheriff Dalton didn't dismiss her charges as nonsense. She could have sworn she even heard a thread of concern in his voice. He promised to meet her at the cottage right after he stopped at the cemetery. When she was certain she wasn't being followed, she headed back to the cottage.

In the short time it took her to drive back, her confidence level had returned. She'd been faced with a serious problem and she hadn't panicked. She'd kept her head and done the right thing.

When Sophie pulled up in her driveway, she immediately noted that Sheriff Dalton wasn't the only visitor to her cottage today. Her eyes lit on a brightly wrapped present resting on the porch floor by her front door.

Cain.

Her emotions tumbled. She was disappointed that she'd missed him. Every fiber of her being wanted to run to him, feel his arms wrap around her, hear the steady beat of his heart beneath her ear, calming her, offering her a safe haven.

But in a way she was glad she'd missed him. She was no longer his responsibility and she was determined to see this through on her own. After all, Sheriff Dalton couldn't be far behind. And, hopefully, when she saw Cain again, she'd be able to tell him everything. No more omissions. Everything out in the open. And she and the sheriff might actually have a plan of action regarding what the next step should be.

Ever vigilant, Sophie sat in the car a moment longer, scanning the property, assuring herself she'd be safe—and alone— if she opened her door. Once she was certain no one lurked in the bushes, she hurried to the front door, lifted the gift from the floor, unlocked the dead bolts and let herself into the house. Immediately, she turned and reset the locks. She glanced out the curtains. She was safe and the sheriff was on his way.

She plopped down on the sofa and turned her attention to the present on her lap. A big yellow bow and lovely flowered paper covered the flat, rectangular box. She slid her fingernail along the edge, broke the seal and lifted the lid.

A box of chocolates.

She popped one into her mouth, almost salivating when

the gooey center and the rich dark chocolate hit her taste buds. She had hoped Cain would come back once he had had a chance to think things over, once he realized being fired hadn't ended things between them, but just opened the door for future possibilities. They were matching puzzle pieces. A perfect fit. It just took him a little longer to figure that out.

Sophie indulged herself and popped a second piece of candy into her mouth. She couldn't wait to see him again. She had so much to tell him.

Before she'd finished the second piece, her vision began to blur and her fingertips started to tingle. What was happening? She tried to stand but her legs felt like blocks of cement and they refused to move. Her arms fell to her sides and the unexpected dead weight caused her to topple over on the sofa.

I've been poisoned. Dear Lord, help me, please.

Her mind was still sharp and she did her best not to panic. She needed to reach her bag and retrieve her cell phone but her arm wouldn't obey her mind's commands. She lay sprawled on the sofa like a mannequin unable to move.

Think, Sophie. Think.

She could feel her heart hammering and her breath came in quick, short gulps.

I'm wide awake but I can't make my body move. I haven't been poisoned. I've been drugged.

A bottle stuffed with a burning rag crashed through the front window and rolled across the carpet. To Sophie's horror it set everything in its path on fire.

Instinctively, she tried to scream and became even more terrified when she was unable to utter a sound. Her throat muscles must have been paralyzed. She couldn't scream for help, not that anyone could hear her. For the first time in her life, Sophie regretted living so far from town.

A second bottle flew through the window and within seconds the curtains were engulfed in flames.

Although her body refused to work, her mind was not yet affected and she was still able to think. She tried desperately to calm herself.

Don't be afraid. Sheriff Dalton's on his way.

But he'd told her he was stopping at the cemetery first. Sophie's stomach lurched when she realized that it would be impossible for him to reach her in time. She was alone—and she was going to die.

Heavy black, noxious smoke filled the room, seeping into her lungs, stealing what breath she had left, and her frozen throat muscles refused to cough any of it out. The intensity of the fire's heat scorched her face as the flames inched closer. Shooting embers fell on the sofa and it started to smolder. Embers landed on her skin, burning her, and she couldn't move to brush them away.

As the smoke entered her body she began to feel woozy, disoriented. The room started to spin. She could almost feel the life trickling out of her body. Resigned to the inevitability of her imminent death, Sophie began to pray.

Dear Lord, please forgive me for my sins. Wrap me in Your loving arms and carry me home. But, please, Lord I have just one request. Don't let Cain think any of this is his fault. Don't let him punish himself for leaving last night. Please, God, don't let him think our relationship was his mistake number two.

Accepting the knowledge that her time on this earth was slipping away and that she had made her peace with God, she stopped fighting and allowed her mind and body to drift in and out of consciousness. She closed her eyes and began humming "Amazing Grace" in her mind.

A deafening crash mixed simultaneously with the shattering of glass came in the direction of her bedroom in the back of the cottage. Sophie's eyes, the last thing still obeying her mind's commands, opened.

A dark figure of a man loomed in the bedroom doorway, looking around, getting his bearings, and then he headed right for her.

Her heart leapt for joy. She was being rescued.

Sheriff Dalton?

No. Even hunched over against the heat and flames as he made his way toward her, she knew from the slimness of his build that it wasn't the sheriff.

Cain?

She took a long, hard look. It wasn't Cain. She'd know his build, his gait, anywhere.

When she realized it wasn't either man, a lone tear slid down her cheek. *It must be a member of the crime family.* They'd kept their promise. They were here to finish the job. The image of the headstone flashed through her mind.

Sophia Joy Gimmelli…Time's Up…R.I.P

By now flames engulfed most of the living room. Fingers of fire danced across the ceiling, but still the man lumbered toward her.

Idiot. Why risk your life? Won't I be dead soon enough for you?

The man held a white rag against his nose and mouth in an obvious attempt to protect his lungs from the thick black waves of smoke billowing throughout the cottage. He leaned forward, bending low at the waist. With the other arm extended to protect his head from falling debris, he dodged the furniture in his path and continued moving toward her.

Sophie didn't know if the tiny puffs of air she was able to pull into her lungs could even count as breath. Her chest constricted with pain as her lungs fought back against the lack of oxygen. The acrid odor coated the inside of her nostrils. Her tongue thickened and the back of her throat burned.

Seconds. Although it seemed like an eternity, Sophie knew only seconds had passed from the first time the flaming bottle had come through the window until now. Seconds—stretching in slow motion to minutes.

Still unable to move, she watched helplessly as the man reached the sofa. As he towered over her, Sophie looked up and stared into his eyes.

Oh…Lord…

SEVENTEEN

Thank you, Lord.

Sophie's father was alive. Dominic Gimmelli was here, standing over her, trying to save her. But was it too late for both of them?

Her father stooped down to pick her up when a large chunk of ceiling broke away, collapsed onto his back and knocked him to the ground.

No! Please, God, no! Her mind screamed and her eyes widened as she searched the rubble for signs he was still alive.

A shift of debris. Then another. Dominic struggled from beneath the burning material and sat up. His hair and shirt were on fire. Immediately he rolled back and forth against the floor to extinguish the flames licking at his shirt. He slapped out the wisps of fire in his hair with his bare hands. Coughing and weakened but still alive, he got back on his feet and quickly scooped Sophie into his arms.

She wanted to wrap her arms around his neck. She wanted to hold tight and never let him go. But her useless, paralyzed arms hung lifelessly at her sides, weighing her down.

The roar of the fire was deafening. The flames crackled and spit almost like a living, breathing animal as the wooden walls and floor became nothing more than kindling to the already out-of-control fire. The entire front of the cottage, engulfed in an impenetrable wall of flame, loomed before them, blocking their exit. Their only hope of escape was through the back of the house.

Dominic struggled with Sophie's cumbersome, motionless body. He tried to carry her and, when he buckled beneath her dead weight, he clasped her against his body, half pulling, half dragging her with him. He staggered, knocked into a table, caught himself and took another step.

As they passed the bookshelf, Sophie saw him spot her treasure box, the childhood possession he'd hand-carved for her and which he knew she'd cherished. Sophie had filled that box with bits and pieces of memories and dreams, and it was the only constant that had stayed with her throughout the hundreds of moves through hundreds of small towns. Now she didn't care about the box. All she cared about was her father.

Her father snatched it from the shelf.

Let it go, Dad! We need to get out of here. I don't care about the box. Please.

Her mind screamed the words but she knew she hadn't uttered a sound.

Still paralyzed from the drugs and succumbing quickly to smoke inhalation, Sophie drifted in and out of consciousness. She fought with every fiber of her being to remain conscious, as though somehow staying awake would be the emotional support her father needed to save them.

Her father was alive…and back in her life. They couldn't die now.

Please, God. Not now. Not yet. Please.

The hard edges of the box now nestled between them cut into Sophie's rib cage. She winced as a sharp point pierced through her clothes and into her skin.

Why didn't he drop it? Why didn't he concentrate on just getting the two of them out of this inferno?

She could hear his heavy grunts and labored breathing as he continued to slowly move toward the back of the cottage.

As they approached the kitchen, the gases in the ceiling materials ignited creating a flashover. The sudden explosion of flames knocked them backward. Sophie's face slammed into the kitchen doorjamb. She didn't need the thick, wet stream of blood flowing over her lips to tell her she'd broken her nose. Crushed against the wood, her face slid down the jamb, splinters deeply imbedding themselves in her cheek, until her body collapsed onto the wood floor.

Dad?

Unable to raise her head to look for him, panic seized her heart.

Where is he? Where?

Two arms snaked around her from behind and hefted her up.

Still alive. Oh, thank you, Lord, he's still alive.

A wave of flames radiated down on the room in front of them, trapping them, blocking all possibility of making it out the back door. Their only means of escape now was through the bedroom. As though he could read her mind, her father immediately turned toward her room, stumbled, righted himself and stumbled again.

Twenty feet to freedom.

The next stumble dropped them both to the ground. Dominic Gimmelli rose to his knees and stayed there. Critical seconds ticked by but the man seemed unable to move. Finally, shoulders heaving as he struggled to take in air, he got to his feet, wrapped his arms around Sophie and moved toward the opening he had crashed through where her bedroom window used to be.

Fifteen feet.

He fell again. This time unable to get up. Dominic began to crawl. He dragged and pulled them both across the hardwood floor.

Ten feet.

Her father was a brave, fit man but the fire was proving to be an insurmountable opponent that he could not conquer. Sophie sensed the moment he gave up. He stopped crawling, stopped moving. Then, slowly, as if his movements took massive effort, he sat up, wrapped her in his arms and simply waited.

Sophie felt an inner calmness, a peace wash over her as she accepted the inevitability of their death. Her heart offered up a silent prayer.

Heavenly Father, I sense Your loving presence even now. I thank You, Lord, for returning my father to me and allowing us to find solace in each other's arms as You prepare to bring us both home.

Sophie's face rested against her father's cheek as he cradled her in his arms. Their eyes caught and held. His face, covered in black soot and ash, glistened in the firelight with sweat and tears. She tried with every remaining ounce of strength she possessed to send him a message with her eyes. To let him know how much she loved him…how grateful she was she'd had him for a father…to say goodbye.

Unable to cling to consciousness any longer, Sophie slipped into the darkness.

Smoke. Thick black plumes of smoke funneled from the ground to the sky like a tornado touching earth.

Cain leaned his chest against the steering wheel so he could get a better look at the horizon through the car's windshield and couldn't believe his eyes. It was definitely smoke— and it was coming from the direction of Sophie's house. He slammed his foot on the accelerator, pushing the speedometer to its limit and, as his car lurched forward, he grabbed his cell phone and dialed 911.

Cain's heart hammered in his chest and his pulse raced as he turned off the main highway onto the dirt road leading to Sophie's cottage. Even from this distance, the acrid smell of smoke seeped into the car and filled his nostrils. He coughed repeatedly against the noxious fumes and, in a panic to get to Sophie, drove faster.

Within minutes, he'd pulled in front of the cottage and jumped out of his car the second he had slammed it into park.

Cain looked in horror at the scene before him. Sophie's porch and the entire front wall of her home were now an angry, burning, yellow wall of flame. Dense inky smoke billowed to the sky and swirled in poisonous vapors around him.

Sophie.

He saw her car parked by the shed.

Oh, Lord, no! Please...don't let Sophie be inside that inferno.

"Sophie!" He screamed her name but his voice was lost in the overwhelming roar of the fire.

Cain, yelling her name with every step, raced to the back of the cottage. He sprinted around the corner of the house and his legs almost collapsed beneath him when he was confronted by an equally destructive, impenetrable wall of flame.

He was too late. There was no way anyone could still be alive inside that inferno. And on the outside chance she was alive, he prayed she'd be unconscious and not aware, not terrified as the fire approached—because there was no way anyone could rescue her.

His stomach lurched. He bent at the waist and retched.

He'd lost two women he loved. He failed them both—Lucy, Sophie—gone because he failed them. Pain seized his chest like an iron fist had clamped onto his heart, and he dropped to his knees.

Sophie. Forgive me. I should never have left you last night.

Cain heard a siren in the distance but the sound offered him little solace. They were too late. He was too late. Tears fell freely down his face and, in a fleeting moment of weakness, he contemplated rushing into the flames, because without Sophie he would be dead anyway.

Stop thinking with your emotions and think with your head! A strong voice inside his head commanded his attention. *Keep looking. Circle the house. Find a way in.*

Cain immediately circled the house. The incredible heat seared his face. His clothes felt like they were melting on his body but still he crouched close to the perimeter of the house, looking, searching for even the tiniest spot not engulfed in flame—and then he saw it.

A hole in the wall, remnants of broken glass indicating it had been a back window. The opening had not yet been consumed by the quickly encroaching fire. Cain leaned from the waist up through the hole and, again, screamed Sophie's name. He cupped his hand against his eyes and tried to peer through the smoke. At first, he couldn't see much of anything, but once his eyes adjusted he could make out a chest of drawers and a little farther inside the room a double bed. Crumpled in a heap beside the bed was a lump of—something.

"Over here." A man's voice, hoarse and barely audible amid the crackling of the fire, reached Cain's ears. He didn't need a second invitation to clamber inside. He ignored the broken shards of glass slicing his skin and ran toward the sound.

Cain found two bodies huddled together on the floor beside

the bed. The man—someone Cain had never seen before—shifted out of the way and weakly gestured toward the body on the floor.

Sophie.

Cain's body doubled uncontrollably with coughing spasms and the acrid smoke burned his eyes but nothing could stop him from drawing her into his arms. Eyes closed, she hung lifelessly in his arms. Barely able to breathe, he knew he had mere seconds to get her out of here before both of them would be lost forever to either the smoke or the flames that were now eating away at her bedroom door.

His eyes met those of the older man on the floor, who was too weak to stand or even speak but managed to gesture with his hand for them to go. Cain stood up, lifting Sophie in his arms and ran with her toward the bedroom window.

Just as he reached the opening, Sheriff Dalton appeared in the window. He reached out his arms to take Sophie. Cain transferred her into the sheriff's arms and then turned and raced back inside to try and rescue the man. The bedclothes were aflame and sparks had fallen on the man's body. Small fingers of fire began eating at his clothes, but the man was too weak to care.

Cain slapped his hands up and down the man's arms and legs, extinguishing the fire. He grabbed him under his arm pits and dragged him to the window. Sheriff Dalton helped Cain lift the man through the opening and not a moment too soon. The three men had barely cleared the structure when the ceiling of the bedroom collapsed and a whoosh of flame shot through the window and flashed up into the sky.

Sheriff Dalton, the rescued man and Cain collapsed beneath a tree a safe distance from the blaze.

Fire trucks barreled up the dirt road and pulled in front of the roaring inferno. The house was a lost cause. Now it became imperative to keep the flames contained and not allow them to reach the woods surrounding the property.

Cain's eyes darted around him until he saw Sophie lying a few feet farther away. He scrambled to her side, lifting her head and cradling it with his left arm while his right hand felt for a pulse in her neck. All the air gushed out of him in relief when he felt a slow, but steady, beat beneath his fingers.

"Sophie?" He called her name but she remained unresponsive.

A paramedic dropped to his knee beside them. "I'll take over now, sir." The paramedic reached out to lift Sophie from his arms but Cain found he couldn't let her go. He'd come so close to losing her forever—too close.

"Hey, buddy, you've got to let go and let us help her."

Reluctantly, Cain released his grasp. Within moments, she'd been transferred to a gurney. One paramedic had fastened an oxygen mask to her face and was taking her vitals while a second paramedic left them to check on the condition of the sheriff and the rescued man.

Cain moved behind the gurney to stay out of the way but still remain close by. He brushed soot and ash from Sophie's hair. When he noted the slow but steady rise and fall of her chest, he couldn't hold back his emotions and he choked on a sob.

Thank you, God.

Sophie was alive.

Sounds bombarded Sophie's ears. Men's voices…loud but too far away for her to understand their words. Gushing water. Engines. The thunderous pounding of feet running past her. Equipment moving.

She tried to open her eyes but her lids wouldn't budge.

She drew in a deep breath and then another before she realized she had a mask pressed against her face. She tried to lift her hand to feel the mask but her arms were strapped down.

Someone clasped her fingers in a firm, hard grasp.

"Sophie?" That one simple word was filled with worry and anguish.

She blinked. Once. Twice. Then forced her eyelids open. *Cain*.

Streaks of black coated his face. His hair dripped with water, his T-shirt was drenched and plastered to his chest.

Where was her father? Had she imagined him? Had it been Cain who saved her life?

Sophie's attempt to speak came out as nothing more than a harsh, guttural sound.

"Shh. Try not to talk."

"That's right, miss." A second man dressed in a medical uniform moved into her peripheral vision. "You've damaged your throat. We won't know how severely until you're examined at the hospital."

Sophie wiggled her fingers and a wave of relief washed over her that she wasn't still paralyzed.

"Try to rest, Miss Gimmelli. Your father told us you'd been given a muscle paralytic," the paramedic said. "We gave you a shot to counteract the symptoms but it's going to take some time before it takes full effect."

Her father? Then she hadn't imagined it. He was alive.

She was able to turn her head and look in the direction of her cottage.

Gray smoke oozed off the smoldering embers that had once been her home.

The yard buzzed with activity. Fire trucks and police cars were parked haphazardly across what had been her lawn. Firemen trampled everywhere, including through the last remnants of her rose garden. One man talked on a handheld walkie-talkie as he passed. Some sifted through the ashes. Others busied themselves winding up lengths of hose.

"Hang in there, Miss Gimmelli. We'll load you in the bus in a second." The paramedic adjusted the IV he'd inserted into her left arm and then stepped a few feet away.

Sophie blinked against the flashing red lights of the ambulance. Her eyes shot to Cain and she tried, again, to speak.

"Dad…?" Unbearable pain seared the lining of her throat but at least she'd been able to produce an audible word.

"Shh, Sophie, please. Don't talk."

He must have seen the thousands of questions in her eyes because he stroked her hair and started to speak.

"Your dad's okay. The paramedics are with him now. He's got some first- and second-degree burns but he'll be fine. As soon as they dress his wounds, you'll both be on your way to the emergency room."

Cain closed his eyes for a second. His lips barely moved and Sophie knew he was praying. When he opened his eyes, a wave of relief seemed to wash over him.

"It was the Lord, Sophie. Directing my path. Helping me find you before it was too late." His words faltered as he relived the terror of the last few moments.

Cain lifted her hand and kissed her fingertips and chuckled. "It was a close call. Too close. Maybe someday we'll look back on this and laugh because watching Sheriff Dalton try to pull your father out of the building…well, let's just say it's an image I won't soon forget. Your father insisted on holding on to that treasure chest he carved for you. I thought Dalton was going to hit your dad over the head with it. Almost did, in fact. The box was in pieces but your dad just wouldn't let it go."

Sophie's eyes glanced around the ground.

"Here it is." Cain held up the remains of what once had been her treasure chest.

Sophie stared at the pieces of wood in Cain's hands and blinked in surprise when she realized that there had been not one, but *two,* secret hiding places built into the box. But now, the box was empty—nothing remained but smashed, splintered pieces of wood.

Cain followed her gaze. "We were right, Sophie. Your dad did hide his evidence against the Mob in your treasure chest. You and I found the drawer built into the lid. What we didn't suspect when we checked it out the first time was that he had built a second hiding place, a false bottom, into the chest." Cain chuckled. "Your dad fought Dalton like a tiger to save it, too. He wasn't about to let it go up in flames."

Cain ran his palm over her head. "The evidence is intact, Sophie. It's been turned over to the federal marshals and everything's going to be okay."

Everything's going to be okay. That has to be Cain's favorite expression because he says it over and over again.

Sophie closed her eyes and squeezed another breath of clean, pure oxygen into her lungs.

It is over. Finally, over.

Sophie darted her eyes around the yard and then looked back at Cain with a question in her eyes.

"Dalton?" he asked, probably knowing that he'd accounted to her for everyone else.

"He spotted someone running away. He and a couple of his men grabbed their rifles and took off a few minutes ago like foxes on a rabbit hunt."

Two paramedics appeared again at her side. "Time to go, Miss Gimmelli. We need to get you to the hospital." One of the men squatted down, released the latch on the gurney and raised it three feet from ground level when something zinged off the metal at the gurney's wheel.

Less than a second later a second zing resulted in a bullet lodged in the ambulance's open door.

There'd been two men following her in the black sedan. Sheriff Dalton was after one of them. But now…

She had to warn Cain. But before she could utter a sound, he'd already left.

Cain grabbed a pistol out of the glove compartment of his car and raced in the direction of the shots fired. As he ran into the woods, branches slapped his face and arms. The underbrush wrapped around his ankles and threatened to trip him with each step.

But he'd spent his childhood exploring the woods surrounding Promise and the experience served him well. He paused, staying low and perfectly still as he listened for what direction his opponent had gone. The man he tracked was crashing through the brush, moving haphazardly, sounding like an elephant on a rampage and making it very easy for Cain to locate him and follow.

He knew he should feel exhausted—totally spent both emotionally and physically—but anger pulsed through his body and pure adrenaline kept him moving forward, stealthily, cautiously, as he circled around and actually found himself ahead of the person he was tracking.

Cain watched the man approach. The shooter kept glancing over his shoulder as he stumbled and pushed his way through the brush.

Cain waited for him to draw closer. When the man was within easy firing range, Cain threw a rock, creating a loud echoing crack as it connected with a tree about twenty feet to their left.

The shooter spun toward the sound and fired three times in succession.

Cain stood up and fired once.

The man yelled, the impact spinning him around, and he fell to the ground clutching his shoulder.

Cain was on him in a minute, grabbing the weapon out of his hand and standing on his extended arm. The shooter tried to sit up but Cain placed the barrel of his weapon against his forehead. "Go ahead. Give me a reason to squeeze this trigger."

The man lay back down, raising his other arm over his head.

More crashing through brush sounded in the woods. When Cain turned his head, Deputy Blake appeared on the scene, gun drawn. He gestured Cain away, forced the suspect on his stomach and handcuffed his hands behind his back.

"Good job. The sheriff has the other guy cuffed and sitting in the back of his patrol car." Blake dragged the suspect to his feet and the three of them headed back in the direction they'd come.

Sheriff Dalton met them at the edge of the woods. He read the suspect his rights and guided him into the backseat of the squad car, where his partner, already handcuffed, waited.

Cain looked for Sophie and was just in time to see the taillights of the ambulance disappear in the distance.

EIGHTEEN

The nurse entered Sophie's private hospital room—which didn't seem private. There'd been a steady stream of staff and visitors. It was the twenty-four-hour police guard sitting outside her door screening everyone that entered that made Sophie skittish.

They'd caught the arsonists, hadn't they? So why the police guard?

Cain had told her that the sheriff had arrested the suspected arsonist, who had tried to flee the scene, as well as the fellow that had shot at them. Knowing that he had always been afraid that he wouldn't be able to trust his leg to do what he wanted in a crisis, it had held up just fine during the pursuit. Sophie smiled remembering the look on his face when he'd repeated the chase scene to his parents and Holly—indulging in a little well-deserved boasting during the tale.

The sheriff had the men in custody. The evidence had been turned over to the federal marshals. Tape recordings implicating individuals in his father's crime family to loan sharking and murder. Copies of fraudulent accounts covering up their money laundering. It was over, wasn't it? So why were there guards at her door?

Sophie couldn't help the feeling of dread in her stomach that the worst was yet to come.

Nurse Crabtree approached the bed. The woman's name never failed to get a smile out of Sophie. No one could be less like their name. She'd been nothing but kind, friendly and helpful—she'd even bent the rules and allowed Cain to stay well past the limited visiting hours. Last night when he had been standing by her bed to say good-night, Nurse Crabtree had grinned at Sophie, made a thumbs-up gesture behind Cain's back and mouthed the words, "He's a hunk." Sophie had barely suppressed her laughter.

"Now, remember what I told you," the nurse said as she approached the bed with a mirror and brush in her hand. "It's not as bad as it looks." She held the mirror against her chest. "I'm going to give you a quick peek and then I'll go get your discharge papers. But I don't want you getting yourself all upset. Everything you see…*everything*…will heal."

Sophie, fully dressed and sitting on the edge of the bed, inhaled deeply. She must look even worse than she thought because Nurse Crabtree had spent the better part of the past fifteen minutes assuring her that it wasn't that bad. What was that old saying about protesting too much?

"Your nose was broken. You needed several stitches when the doctor removed some deeply embedded wooden slivers from your left cheek. Your right cheek has a significant burn, which will probably require a skin graft, but we have two excellent plastic surgeons on staff."

Plastic surgeons? Ohh, this was quickly going from bad to worse.

"Smoke inhalation caused some swelling, puffiness and even some discoloration in your face," the nurse continued. "That will probably be what bothers you the most." She patted her hand in an effort to reassure her. "But everything will heal and you'll be good as new in no time."

The nurse looked Sophie in the eye. "Ready?"

Sophie nodded.

But she wasn't ready. She would never have been ready to see the monster mask that stared back at her. With trembling fingers she took the mirror from the nurse's hand and brought it closer.

Two blackened, purplish eyes stared back at her. A wide, white bandage covered her nose. Her lips—cracked and horribly swollen—resembled a collagen procedure gone bad. And her skin. The nurse hadn't been wrong about that. Sophie didn't know which looked worse, the dark stitches running diagonally across her left cheek, the gauze covering the right side of her face or the nasty, mottled coloring of her skin. She barely recognized her own reflection.

Slowly, she raised her other hand and touched her hair— what she had left of it. Several sections of hair had been burned away leaving scattered bald spots across her scalp. What had once been shiny, long ebony strands of her hair had been broken off, many of the ends singed by the heat. Now lifeless, drab hair framed her face like a hanging tattered rag.

Tears seeped from the corners of her eyes. Sophie blinked in surprise as she stared into the mirror and watched the liquid seep into the bandages on her face. She thought you had to be human to cry, but this couldn't be a human face, could it?

The nurse placed a hand gently on her shoulder. She spoke softly and tried to comfort her. "I know it's a shock…but it isn't permanent." She dabbed a tissue against Sophie's eyes. "I promise. Each day the swelling will lessen. Hair grows back. Bandages come off." She leaned over and made eye contact with her. "It could have been worse, Sophie. Try to remember that."

The nurse's words humbled her. She was right. God had spared her life. And none of her injuries were life threatening or permanent. She needed to give her human nature a kick in the pants and offer up some prayers of gratitude.

But her human nature was winning at the moment. She couldn't stop her thoughts from flying to Cain. He'd spent most of the past twenty-four hours by her side. The entire time he'd never given her the slightest hint—not one wince or grimace or comment that he had been looking at a monster.

And Holly and Mrs. Garrison—they'd both come to visit. They'd been upbeat, positive, teasing.

Holly had even cracked one joke after another. "Just to see if those collagen lips of yours can move," she'd said. "Can you imagine that some people pay thousands of dollars to beef those puppies up and you got them for free?"

Thinking about it, Sophie realized that mother and daughter were old pros at keeping the look of horror out of their eyes. They'd had to do it for over a year and a half during Cain's rehabilitation.

Her tears flowed freely now. She would never have let them visit if she'd realized how horrific she looked—not just to avoid her own embarrassment but to spare them their painful memories.

"Are you okay?"

Sophie nodded.

"Good girl. I knew you could handle it." Nurse Crabtree patted her shoulder. "I'll be back in as soon as the doctor signs your discharge papers."

Sophie took another glance in the mirror as the nurse slipped out of the room. She was surprised she was being discharged so soon. Was she really doing well enough to go home?

Unable to inhale deeply without pain, she kept her breaths to short, shallow pants. Still suffering from the effects of the damage from smoke inhalation, the back of her throat felt like it had been rubbed raw with sandpaper and her voice was nothing more than a painful, hoarse whisper.

She hadn't been allowed to see her father yet but had been assured by the hospital staff that he was safe and doing well. Dominic Gimmelli had been lucky—his injuries consisted of a few first- and second-degree burns, multiple bruises, smoke inhalation and exhaustion.

But he was alive.

God was good. He'd not only returned her father to her but had protected them both and gotten them out of that inferno alive. She bowed her head and offered up a prayer of thanksgiving.

Sophie put the mirror down and shut her eyes. She was grateful to be alive—truly she was—but her face...

She fought the waves of self-pity tormenting her and, again, tried to turn a positive spin on the situation. She was alive. Her father was alive. The worst was behind her—right?

The rise and fall in the volume of the hospital's paging system combined with a sudden whoosh of air told her someone had just entered the room. She didn't want to see anybody right now. She might never want to see anybody ever again. Resigning herself to the fact that nobody cared what she wanted, she turned her head and opened her eyes.

"Dad!"

Sophie's eyes drank in every inch of him, noting the bandages on his hands and arms, the swelling and bruising on his face, even the bald spot on the left side of his scalp where he was missing a thick patch of hair. But, all in all, he looked fine. He looked better than fine. He was alive and standing in her hospital room instead of residing in the grave she had more than once imagined him in over the past month.

Dominic Gimmelli, accompanied by two men in suits, approached her bed.

"Hello, princess." He wrapped his arms around her and held her tight.

"Some princess," she whispered hoarsely as she moved out of his hold and lay back on the bed. "How can you stand looking at me?"

He leaned closer, his face mere inches from hers, and locked his eyes with hers. "That's all I want to do, honey. Look at you. Be with you. Having to leave you behind was one of the most difficult decisions I've ever had to make." He clasped her hand. "But it's over now, pumpkin. Everything's going to be fine."

"Over?" Sophie's eyes darted from one of the men beside her father to the other, her unasked question hanging in the air.

"Sophie, these men are federal marshals. Agent Lance Dickerson," he said, indicating the man on his left. "And Agent Tom Broward." Her father turned toward the men. "Can I have a few minutes alone with my daughter?"

"I'm sorry, Mr. Gimmelli. We have strict orders not to leave you out of our sight. For your protection, you understand."

Dominic sighed and nodded.

Agent Broward dragged two straight-back chairs in from the hall and placed them in the far corner of the room. He withdrew a handheld gaming device from his suit pocket, which he handed to his partner and withdrew a small radio with earpieces and a paperback book from the other. "We'll be leaving the hospital just as soon as the medical arrangements are completed. In the meantime, just pretend we're not here."

Dominic Gimmelli nodded at the federal agents and then pulled a chair of his own close to Sophie's bed.

"Leaving? Dad, what are they talking about?"

"Shh, it's okay, Sophie. Everything's going to be okay."

Sophie gritted her teeth. First Cain and now her father. If she never heard those lame words again, it would be too soon.

Her father looked older than she remembered. Fatigued. Weary. Defeated. Could four weeks in hiding do this to a person—or were the past twenty-two years on the run finally taking their toll?

"I messed up, Sophie." His face contorted as he tried to hold back tears and he dropped his head. "Can you ever forgive me?"

Pain seized her heart. "Dad. Don't." She lifted his chin so she could look him in the eyes. "We're alive...and we're together...and all the rest..." She waved a hand in the air. "All the rest will work itself out."

Her father sat up straight. His eyes glittered with telltale moisture but he had regained control of his emotions.

"You are so much like your mother. I look at you and I see her...in your eyes...the way you tilt your head.... I hear her in your laughter.... She's always there, inside you, shining through you. Thank God you got very little from my gene pool."

Sophie remained quiet, giving her father the time he needed to gather his thoughts, to tell his story in his own way. When she saw him continue to struggle, she prompted him.

"Talk to me, Dad. I'm a big girl. You don't have to protect me anymore. Just talk to me." And then she held her breath and waited.

Before he could speak, a commotion at the door caught their attention. The door cracked open and Sheriff Dalton stuck his head inside. Speaking to the federal agents, who'd looked up when the door opened, he said, "There's someone out here who's being pretty insistent about coming in."

The marshals glanced at one another.

"I'm not trying to tell you guys your business but I'm just

thinkin' it would be easier on all of us to let him in. He's not going away quietly, I can promise you that, and I really don't want to be forced to arrest him."

"Sophie?" The door edged open a bit wider as Cain tried unsuccessfully to shoulder his way past Sheriff Dalton, who did not seem to appreciate Cain trying to squeeze through the doorway without permission and shoved back.

"Cain?" Sophie strained her neck trying to see past her father to the scrimmage scene in the doorway as the two men struggled against each other.

The marshals nodded. With a frown on his face, the sheriff moved to the side and allowed Cain to enter the room.

The aroma of homemade pot roast preceded him as he entered and placed a Styrofoam container on the nearby hospital tray table. Cain gestured toward the package. "It's Tuesday. I thought you might be hungry."

Sophie wanted to laugh. Her lips strained at the effort and the sound was more a chortle than a laugh but, somehow, it was comforting to know that even in the midst of total chaos some things stayed the same—like pot roast day at Holly's diner.

Cain's eyes swept the room. He nodded in the direction of the federal marshals and then turned and offered a hand to her father.

"Mr. Gimmelli," he clasped the older man's hand in his. "It's nice to officially meet you."

"You're the young man that pulled us out of the fire." Dominic Gimmelli took careful assessment of Cain as he returned his handshake.

"Sheriff Dalton and I did, yes, sir."

"I haven't had the chance to thank you."

Their eyes locked and Sophie watched in fascination as they sized each other up. Almost like two dogs sniffing each other, determining territory and deciding to find a peaceful way to share the same turf. She shook her head. *Men are nothing more than tall boys.*

Cain shot a glance at Sophie. "Am I interrupting?"

"Depends." Sophie's father stood up and looked Cain squarely in the face. "I have to ask, son, what makes any of this your business?"

"Dad!" Sophie blurted, "There's no need to be rude. I hired Cain to find you when you disappeared."

Dominic digested the information. "Please don't misunderstand me. I'm grateful for everything you've done for my daughter…and, obviously, for me." He continued to stare at Cain. "But as you can see, I am no longer missing so I am assuming your business with my daughter is over. What is going on in this room is no longer your concern. You're free to leave—with our gratitude, of course."

Cain straightened his shoulders and actually looked like he was digging in his heels. "Sophie is my business, sir. I believe I'll stay awhile."

Sophie sighed audibly. She tried to squeeze a degree of authority into her hoarse, whispery voice. "If the two of you don't start acting like men instead of children, I'm going to throw both of you out on your ears."

The men turned their attention to Sophie.

"I mean it. Haven't we all been through enough?"

Her father had the decency to look chagrined and sat back down in his chair.

"Okay, Dad, time's up. You have a whole lot of explaining to do."

NINETEEN

Dominic Gimmelli cut a glance at Cain and then back to Sophie.

"It's okay," Sophie assured him. "Cain's the one who helped me find out most of the information anyway."

Her father mumbled under his breath and squirmed beneath their scrutiny as Sheriff Dalton and both federal marshals joined the circle at Sophie's bed. If Dominic had hoped to have a private, intimate conversation with his daughter it wasn't going to happen. Sighing heavily, he clasped Sophie's hands and locked his gaze with hers.

"I was a guest teacher at the local college the summer I met your mother. I didn't realize, at first, that she was seventeen. I automatically assumed if she was taking a college course she was older. I didn't realize anyone can enroll in a summer art class." He shrugged, a sheepish grin evident on his face.

"Elizabeth owned the sun—and it radiated from inside her. She had a zest for life, an exuberance and curiosity that was contagious. She was quick-witted, intelligent…challenging." A ghost of a smile touched his lips. "I had never met anyone like her." He gently touched the side of Sophie's face. "And no matter what else you come to believe about me, Sophia, know this…I loved your mother. She owned my heart…and always will."

Sophie's eyes glistened with tears. She placed her fingers on top of the hand he held against her cheek and, for that single moment in time, it was just the two of them, bonding, remembering, sharing an intimacy the others could only witness, not feel.

"Get to the part about your crime-boss daddy," Sheriff Dalton said, shifting his weight and crossing his arms over his chest. "If you think I'm gonna stand here and listen to this romantic fairy tale you're painting, you're wrong."

The sheriff glared at Sophie's father. "As far as I can tell the facts should speak for themselves, don't ya think, Gimmelli? And the fact is you're prince to the throne of the Maryland-based crime family. Isn't that right?"

He puffed out his chest and planted his hands on his hips. "Want to hear another fact? How about the fact that you came into our community and took up with a young, innocent teenager from one of our town's most prominent families. That young girl didn't know the first thing about corruption, loan sharks and executions. But you did, didn't you? And you took that little girl away from her home, ruined her life and caused her murder. How's that for facts, Gimmelli? Doesn't sound so fairy-tale romantic now, does it?"

Sophie gasped at the harshness of the sheriff's words.

The color drained from her father's face as he stared at the sheriff in silence. When he turned his attention back to Sophie, the pain she saw in his eyes broke her heart.

"Don't you talk to my father like that." Despite the pain, Sophie yelled at the sheriff. "Get out! You don't need to be here and I want you to leave. Now!"

Her father patted her shoulder and tried to calm her. "Sophia, stop. I can understand the sheriff's point of view. The facts are the facts. I am Dominic Gimmelli, the only son of Vincent Gimmelli. And he ran one of the largest and strongest crime families in Maryland." Her father shrugged.

"I wish I could deny it. I wish I could claim to be the son of an accountant or a teacher or even a farmer, maybe. But we're born into our families, Sophia. We don't choose them…and we don't choose the baggage they come with." He smiled at her. "As you are finding out for yourself.

"Most of my childhood," he continued, "I believed my father was a well-respected and powerful businessman. When I grew old enough to understand the nature of my father's empire, I confronted him, disowned him…told him to his face just how much I hated him." A deep sadness entered his eyes. "But I didn't hate him. I loved him. He was my papa, after all."

Sophie understood all too well her father's mixed emotions.

"My father sent me to live abroad. He kept me as far removed from his business ties as possible. When I returned to the United States, I took the job teaching at the college in Promise. I met your mother, fell in love, fully intended to spend the rest of my days raising a family right here in Promise."

A shadow darkened his expression. "But the sins of my father followed me here, brought rumors and gossip, brought federal marshals seeking my cooperation in destroying the man who'd given me life."

Dominic dragged his hands over his face, his anguish painfully evident. No one in the room moved or made a sound.

"Your mother made me promise to do the right thing. She convinced me that innocent people were being hurt and I had the power to help them. So I did—not right away, but I did."

Dominic sat back in his chair, his tone of voice resigned, almost robotic, as he recapped the rest of the story.

"I had names, dates, copies of records, taped phone conversations, everything the law would need to destroy my father's empire. I contacted the U.S. Marshals and entered the witness protection program." Tears streamed down Dominic's face. "It was the biggest mistake I ever made."

"Dad…" Sophie reached out to embrace him but he waved her away.

"I trusted them to protect us. I don't know what I was thinking. I knew my father…his ruthlessness…his power… his rage. I knew his contacts and that he'd go to any lengths for revenge. And he did….

"Your mother and I thought we were safe, that we'd beaten him at his own game, that we could live the happy-ever-after life I'd been promising Elizabeth that we'd share."

His eyes looked dark and empty.

"The last time I saw Elizabeth she was smiling at me, waving her hand, laughing and calling out for me to meet her out front—and then she was gone…an explosion…a wall of flames…"

Tears flowed freely down his face. "I tried to get her out. I ran to the car and I put my arms in the fire and I tried…" His eyes pleaded with her to understand. "I tried, Sophia. I tried."

"I know, Dad." She stood up and wrapped her arms around him, offering whatever comfort she could.

Sheriff Dalton shifted uncomfortably. One of the federal marshals coughed. Cain placed a comforting hand on Sophie's shoulder as she embraced her father.

When Sophie stepped back, her father looked into her face.

"You were the only thing I had left of your mother and I needed to protect you at all costs. I no longer trusted the witness protection program. If my father's people found us once, they could find us again. So I took matters into my own hands."

"You ran?" Sophie asked.

"No. I went to see my father."

Sophie gasped. From the sudden tension in the room, it was obvious this new turn of events impacted the other occupants of the room as well.

"Making a deal with Vincent Gimmelli was the only chance I had to keep you alive. With your mother gone, I may as well have been a dead man anyway. I arranged a private meeting with him."

"What happened? Why didn't he kill you? What was the deal?"

"You were the deal."

Sophie raised an eyebrow but remained silent.

"I knew the enormity of your grandfather's vanity and I played on it. He didn't want to leave this world without an heir. He wanted to be nothing more than a footnote in history. He longed for immortality. And the only way he could achieve that would be to leave a bloodline behind.

"I told him about his only granddaughter…the only bloodline of his that he would ever have. I told him I intended to raise her as an artist…a desire he had once had for himself but had been unable to fulfill…and I promised to send him pictures and updates as you grew. And, of course, I promised to destroy the evidence I had against him."

"So he let you go? Just like that?"

Dominic grimaced. "No. It wasn't quite that easy. I didn't walk away. I crawled—with several broken bones. He had to save face, after all."

"If you made a deal with your father, why did you continue to run?" Cain asked.

"Because I couldn't trust my daughter's life to the word of a mobster—no matter who he was. I made sure I kept my word. I sent letters. Updates. But never from anyplace we'd ever lived. Never from anywhere he'd be able to find us. Just kept enough of my word so he would keep his." Dominic stared at Cain until Cain, seeming to be satisfied with the answer, nodded. "Besides, even if my father kept his word, I didn't want others in his organization who craved power to be able to use us as leverage against him. So I ran…and I hid…." He turned and looked at Sophie. "And I tried to give you the best life I could, princess. I'm sorry, Sophia. Can you ever forgive me?"

"There's nothing to forgive, Dad. You did the best you could. But I don't understand. What happened? Why did you have to run away from me? Why now?"

"My father died."

Sophie blinked hard.

"Not only did that mean our protection was gone but now we'd be a target…or at least I would. I was still the only son, the heir to the empire, and there were several cousins in line that wanted me out of the way. Because of the low profile I'd kept over the years, I didn't think they knew about you. I believed you'd be safer if I got as far away from you as possible. So I ran."

Cain perched on the edge of the bed beside Sophie. "Why did you come to Promise, Mr. Gimmelli? And why didn't you tell Sophie you were here?"

"To protect her. I wasn't sure they knew she existed and I didn't want anyone that was tailing me to make the connection. After the attempted hit-and-run in town and the effort to force the two of you off the road at the cemetery, I knew she was in danger. I couldn't come forward and protect her at the same time. So I watched from a distance and intervened when I could."

"That was you drag racing up there on the mountain?" Sheriff Dalton asked.

"Yes. They were trying to force Cain and Sophie over the edge. I had no choice."

"All those times I thought someone was following me... was it you, Dad?"

"Yes...and no..." Dominic chuckled for the first time since he had begun his story. "Truthfully, Sophie, you had more people watching you than bees buzzing around honey. Cain and his sister Holly were your home team." Dominic gestured at the other men in the room. "Sheriff Dalton and the feds hung back in the shadows."

The men grinned.

"The bad guys followed in the distance tap-dancing around the law...and I followed the bad guys."

The tension in the room eased as they all seemed to contemplate the ridiculousness of the situation.

"Well, it's over now." Sophie sighed.

A shadow crossed Dominic's face.

As if on cue, one of the marshals' cell phone rang. He answered it, murmured a few words and slid the phone back in his pocket.

"The medical arrangements have been finalized, Mr. Gimmelli. It's time to go."

"Go?" Sophie's eyes darted from Agent Broward to her father and back again. "What's he talking about, Dad?"

"Sophie, I've agreed to testify. I've turned the evidence over to the U.S. Marshals' office and they've agreed to place us into protective custody. We're going to give the witness protection program another try."

"What? We?" Her eyes flew to Cain and she wondered if the sudden panic that seized her heart and threatened to close her lungs was evident in her eyes. She knew from the shocked expression on his face that he was experiencing similar feelings.

"Dad, I'm not going anywhere. Promise is my home. I have friends here. I have a job...."

"You don't have a choice, Sophie."

"What?" She began pacing the room. "Of course I have a choice. I don't know anything more about the Gimmelli family than what you just told all of us. I can't testify against anyone. There's no reason for me to have to hide."

"Unfortunately, Ms. Gimmelli, there is," Agent Dickerson said. "Your father is in a key position to bring down the entire Maryland organized crime connection, which, in turn, is a major arm of one of the New York crime families. His life is in grave danger. And we can't take the chance that you could be used as a pawn to influence his testimony. We're taking you into protective custody."

Sophie stopped dead in her tracks. Her stomach plummeted to the floor and her legs wobbled.

No. Please, Lord, no. Don't give me my heart's desire only to turn around and take it all away.

"What if I refuse to go?" The hoarseness in her throat made the words come out in a painful, harsh rush.

"I'm sorry." Agent Broward took a step toward her. "You're a material witness. You don't have a choice."

Tears welled in her eyes.

"How long?" The words were nothing more than a whisper.

"At least for the duration of the trial. A year. Maybe two."

The room started to spin and Sophie stretched out a hand to keep herself from falling.

Instantly, Cain appeared at her side, the strength of his arm supporting her, the warmth of his body cradling her. She felt his lips press against the top of her head.

"I'm so sorry, Sophia." Her father stood in front of her, wringing his hands, barely able to look her in the eye. "I know what this is costing you."

"Do you, Dad?" The words came out harsher than she'd intended but her emotions were spinning wildly out of control.

For the first time in her life she had established roots. She'd built a home complete with a church community, a best friend, a job...and Cain. Now it was being ripped away and there was nothing she could do about it. Could anybody really understand?

Cain looked at the men in the room and asked, "Can Sophie and I have a minute alone?"

"We have a van waiting downstairs," Agent Dickerson said.

"I understand. Just a minute...please."

The marshals glanced at each other and Broward nodded. "Okay, Sheriff Dalton and my partner will take Mr. Gimmelli downstairs. I'll step outside and wait for Ms. Gimmelli." He glanced at his watch. "Five minutes. No more."

Cain nodded and drew Sophie closer as the men exited the room.

"I can't believe this is happening." She looked up into his eyes. She felt like an iron fist clenched her heart. "I don't even get to say good-bye to Holly or your mom."

"I'll explain it all to them."

"Then explain it all to me." She pulled out of his embrace and paced angrily around the room. "Explain why I have to pay the price for my father's mistakes. I love him with all my heart. And I'm so grateful he's alive. But I don't want to leave Promise. I don't want to leave..." She left the word *you* unspoken as she stopped and faced him.

Cain's expression held regret and resignation. "I don't want you to leave either, Sophie." He stepped closer and gently brushed a tattered strand of hair off her face. "I realize now that something special was happening between us. Something beautiful. Something promising."

Sophie swallowed the lump forming in her throat and nodded.

"None of this will last forever. Just until the trial ends."

"But you heard the marshal. It will be a year. Maybe two." Sophie shook her head. "That's a lifetime."

Cain pulled her into his arms. "No, Soph. It's a year…or two…for a chance at a lifetime. And that's worth the wait—at least it is for me."

Her throat closed and she choked back a sob. "You'd wait for me?"

He lowered his head and pressed his lips as gently as possible against her swollen ones. Then he pulled her into his arms and she could hear his heart beating beneath her ear, his words rumbling in his chest.

"God put you in my path, Sophie. I was lost in the past—consumed with guilt and grief and mistrust—and He plopped you right down in front of me and said, 'Here. I've chosen someone to teach you to forgive…to teach you to move on… to teach you to trust people again. Her name is Sophie…treat her right.'"

Sophie chuckled in spite of herself.

After a moment, she raised her eyes to his. "What if I can't come back?" she whispered. "What if something goes wrong and I have to enter the witness protection program permanently?"

"God put us together, Sophie. Let's trust Him to find a way to make it work."

A rap on the door interrupted them. Agent Broward stuck his head inside. "It's time to go."

Sophie turned in the doorway and took one long last look at Cain—the lopsided grin that made her pulse race—the thick wave of chestnut hair that fell across his forehead—the deep brown eyes that spoke to her without words.

"It's going to be okay, Soph."

And for the first time she didn't want to throttle him as he spoke those lame, empty words. She wanted to cling to them and hold them close to her heart. She wanted to carry them with her on this next step of her journey. She wanted to believe that with God all things were possible. She offered a silent prayer and, without looking back because it would hurt too much, she closed the hospital door behind her.

TWENTY

Nineteen Months Later

The autumn air was crisp, cool, hinting at the winter months soon to descend on Promise. The leaves on the trees were a majestic canvas of reds, golds and green. Cain stretched his back and wallowed in the warmth of the late afternoon sun. He'd been pulling weeds, planting mums and laying fresh mulch all along the brick path leading up to the porch steps.

The sound of a car speeding up the dirt road caught his attention and he cupped his hand over his eyes as he watched it approach.

The red convertible, top down and spewing dust everywhere, slammed to a stop just a few feet away from him.

He grinned. "Your timing's perfect. I just finished two hours of weeding."

Holly grinned from her position in the driver's seat. "I'm not stupid. Mom told me what time you left. I gave you just enough time to do all the heavy stuff and then thought I'd drive out here and play hero by offering to help."

"Figures." Cain chuckled, picked up his shovel and empty mulch wrappers and crossed over to the shed. When he returned, Holly was sitting on the top step of the porch. Cain joined her.

"The place looks nice," she said.

"Thanks."

"I still can't believe you bought this place."

Cain lifted an eyebrow. "This conversation again?"

"No. I get it. Sophie's father wanted to sell the property after the fire. You bought it and rebuilt. Just in case. I get it."

Cain scowled at his sister. "But?"

"It's been nineteen months since Sophie left. And according to the newspapers the trials ended seven months ago. That's a long time without any word, Cain."

"You know she can't contact me."

"I know she's not *supposed* to contact me. But there are ways—sneaky ways, but ways. An unsigned postcard. An anonymous phone call. Something. Anything."

Cain stood and brushed his hands against the legs of his jeans. "I'm not having this conversation with you again. You're like a broken record, Holly, and I've had my fill." He turned and crossed the porch to the front door. "If you want some apple cider, you're welcome to come in. There's a fresh batch in the fridge. If you want to sit on the porch, enjoy my garden and rest for a while before driving back to town you're welcome. But if you've driven out here to rehash this same old conversation, then leave."

Holly stood, her hands stuck in the back pocket of her jeans, and faced him. "You never gave up on her. All this time and you still keep thinking she's coming back."

"Holly." Anger laced each syllable of her name.

She pulled her hands out of her pockets and held them up defensively. "No, you don't understand. I'm not criticizing you, Cain. Honestly, I'm not. I'm telling you how cool I think it is, really. Especially now that…"

"Now that what?"

Their conversation was interrupted by the sound of a second car rolling up the drive.

"Is that Mom?" Cain looked at his sister. "What's going on? What are the two of you up to?"

"You'll see." Holly grinned and rocked back and forth on her heels waiting for her mother's car to stop before jumping down the porch steps and racing around to the driver's side of the car. His mother opened the door and got out.

"Hello, Cain."

"Mom." Cain crossed the porch and stood on the top step. "What brings you out this way?"

Someone opened the passenger door of his mother's car and he had to shield his eyes against the sun's glare in order to get a look at the person getting out.

"I thought you might like to meet the new art teacher I just hired," his mother said. "Her name's Emma Holliday and she starts first thing Monday morning."

What's going on? They better not be trying to play match-maker like they did a couple weeks ago, and a few weeks before that. Neither one of them seems to understand the word no.

Cain threw a puzzled look his mother's way and then watched as the woman, wearing a red pullover sweater, jeans, leather boots and a pair of large black sunglasses, approached the porch steps. The sun glistened against her short auburn curls.

"Miss Holliday, welcome to Promise." Cain gestured to the porch behind him. "May I offer you a seat and a cool cup of apple cider before my mother takes you on the long drive *back* to town."

When the woman started up the steps, Cain stormed into the house to get a pitcher of cider and some cups and give himself the precious moments he needed to control his temper.

This was the last straw! He wasn't interested in meeting any new art teacher. He wasn't interested in meeting any new anyone. He was going to ream into both of them as soon as this woman was safely out of earshot.

When he carried the tray back out to the porch, he saw the woman standing on the top step, her back to him and continuing a conversation she was having with his mom and sister below. He placed the tray on the table and cleared his throat. "The cider's nice and cold."

She turned to face him, the sun at her back causing him to squint against the glare.

"I hope you'll like living in Promise. Mom's needed help with her art program for quite a while now. Although I must admit, I'm surprised she hired anyone. I thought she was waiting for someone else to fill the spot." He scowled in his mother's direction but offered his hand to the new hire.

The woman ignored his hand, took a couple of steps toward him and removed her glasses. Sea-foam green eyes stared back at him and Cain's heart stopped beating.

"Hello, Cain."

His eyes studied every inch of her face—noting the subtle differences, a thinner, more delicate nose—a squarer chin—and, of course, auburn curls, not silky ebony strands. But the eyes…and the voice…

He held his breath, not daring to hope.

"Soph…"

"Emma," she instantly corrected. "Emma Holliday. I'm the new art teacher. It's good to meet you."

He raised his arm to shake her hand. It moved with such a heaviness he felt like he was swimming through quicksand but he managed to reach out and clasp the hand she offered.

"Emma's not the only new resident in town," Holly said, sheer glee overflowing in her voice. "Mr. Antonio Petrocco moved to town this morning, too. Set up shop right down the street from Dad's pharmacy. Seems he's a carpenter. Dad's already hired him to put in some new countertops and cabinets in the store."

Cain looked into those beautiful green eyes staring back at him and he knew. Every nerve ending in his body leaped with joy. He couldn't resist and reached out to trace a finger lightly down her cheek. "You remind me of somebody," he whispered.

"I do?"

"Yes. Someone very special to me."

"Is that so?" She stepped closer. "Has she been gone?"

"Yes. She's been gone for a very long time."

"And you've been waiting for her? All this time?"

"I've been waiting every second of every day of my life." He ran his hand down her arm trying to convince himself that she was really here…flesh and blood standing in front of him and not some cruel hallucination.

She reached out and clasped his hand. Her eyes glittered with moisture and her voice was husky.

"Did you miss her?"

His emotions were so raw he thought his throat would seize up on him and not allow a word to escape. "The word *missing* doesn't begin to describe how I've felt. I've spent the last nineteen months of my life going through the motions, keeping myself busy, trying to stay positive until she returned."

Cain dropped her hand and pulled her into his arms. "I existed. I didn't live. I got through it only because I'd fool myself into believing in tomorrow. Tomorrow she'd come through that door. Tomorrow I'd hold her in my arms again. Tomorrow…"

"I understand how you felt." She slowly inched her arms around his waist and stepped closer inside his embrace. "I've loved a man like that. I've spent every minute of every day wishing and praying and hoping I would find myself in his arms again."

"You did?"

She smiled up at him and nodded as a lone tear slid down her cheek.

"How did you get through it?" He shifted his stance, wrapped his left arm around her shoulders, cradling her against him. He waved his other arm in an arc at their surroundings. "I buried myself in work. I built this cottage just as I remembered it. I even added two extra rooms, one as a guest room…or maybe nursery. And one as a workroom. She's an artist. She needs a place to work."

"An artist, huh?"

"I polished the wood floors until they gleamed. I added yellow curtains to the windows because I remembered that she liked the color yellow. And I've spent season after season in the garden tending the flowers. She loved her garden. And I wanted it to be perfect…vibrant and beautiful and blooming when she returned." Cain smiled down at her. "Do you think she'll like it?"

Emma's smile widened. "She'll love it. It's everything she could ever imagine…everything she could ever want."

Cain's expression sobered. "Was it difficult for you? Being away from someone you loved?"

"It was more than difficult. But I prayed a lot. I trusted God to help me find a way back to him. I trusted the man I left behind to care about me enough to wait. And I daydreamed."

"Daydreamed?" Cain hooted with laughter. "Ohh, you've got to tell me about those daydreams."

Emma laughed and then her voice grew soft, her tone tender. "I dreamt that I'd sit on the porch swing with him at my side. I dreamt that I'd take a walk in the evenings and count the stars…with him at my side. I dreamt I'd wade in the cool waters of the lake or sculpt figures out of clay or bake homemade bread in the kitchen…." Her eyes locked with his. "And I dreamt about our life together…the children we'd have…the swing he'd hang from the tree at the end of the porch. I dreamt it all…and he was always by my side."

A choking sound distracted them and a quick glance revealed both Cain's mom and sister standing at the bottom of the porch steps with tears running down their cheeks. "Don't mind us," Holly called out as she wrapped an arm around her mother's shoulders and steered her toward the lake. "We're just going to take a walk down by the water. Catch a breeze. Maybe a fish. We'll take our time."

Holly was yards away when Cain's mother looked back and yelled, "I'll keep Holly out of your hair. Don't worry. You two finish your conversation."

The women disappeared over the rise. Cain pulled her close and lifted her chin so he could look into her eyes. "Tell me more about your dreams."

"I'd rather show you. Day in and day out for the rest of my life."

"These past months I've missed the woman I love so much I thought my heart would break."

"But she's home now." She smiled up at him. "Isn't she?"

Tears burned the back of his eyes. "Thank God."

And he did, for directing his path and blessing his life and keeping His promises…always.

* * * * *

Dear Reader,

It's fun for me to share with my readers how I come up with my story ideas. The particular idea for this book literally began with a dream.

I hardly ever dream—or let's say I am rarely conscious of having had a dream when I wake up. That's why I was so surprised that this time, in that nebulous state between being asleep and being awake, I saw myself reading a letter.

I was even more surprised that the letter didn't disappear from my mind like the wisp of a cloud on the horizon once I did awake. It stayed in my memory long enough for me to run to my computer and type it up.

Then the fun began.

Who wrote the letter? Why was their life in danger? And most of all, who was the unfortunate person receiving this letter and how would it impact her life?

I wondered what it would feel like to have someone you love suddenly disappear. What if they claimed that by the time you received the letter they'd be dead? And how would you cope if the loved one offered up their life to save yours?

When I put myself in the letter recipient's place and tried to think what I would do, I instantly thought of going to the police. Maybe getting a private investigator. When I came up with the idea that everything that woman knew—including her own identity—was a lie, the story came alive.

I hope you enjoy *Double Identity* as much as I enjoyed writing it. I'd love to hear from you. Drop me a line anytime at Diane@dianeburkeauthor.com or send snail mail to Steeple Hill, 233 Broadway, Suite 1001, New York, NY 10279.

Blessings,

Diane Burke

QUESTIONS FOR DISCUSSION

1. Sophia finds herself in a position of questioning her own identity. But don't we all choose different "faces" in this world? What are some of the circumstances you've faced where people may see only one side of you?

2. Sophia has a moment when she questions whether faith is real or just something she was raised to believe. If you were raised from childhood to believe in God, do you remember the circumstances where you chose to believe because of faith and not parental urging?

3. In the beginning of our story, Cain has trust issues. Have you ever found it difficult to trust someone once they've hurt you?

4. Mr. Garrison, Mrs. Garrison and Holly have been a very supportive family. Do you have a supportive family? How do you suggest someone find emotional support if their needs aren't met in their own family?

5. There is a point in the book where Sophia and Cain have to step out in faith and believe God will provide, even when it seems impossible. Have you or someone you know had to trust God when trusting was difficult? What were the results?

6. Sophia must find a way to forgive her father. Is forgiveness easy? Does forgive mean forget?

7. How did faith in God impact the lives and decisions of the characters in this story?

8. As a teenager, Mrs. Garrison felt jealous when her relationship with her best friend changed because of another person. Have you been able to maintain friendships you developed in high school? If so, how did the friendship change over the years?

9. Sophie's father discovered that one lie often leads to another. Lies impacted his entire life and eventually had to be faced head-on anyway. Have you or someone you know ever lied and had it trip you up at a later date?

10. Sophie comes up with a unique way to deal with rebellious teenagers and anger management. What would you do if you had the opportunity to impact a teenager who was in danger of taking a wrong path?

11. What lessons, if any, are you able to take away from this story?

Love Inspired®
SUSPENSE

TITLES AVAILABLE NEXT MONTH

Available April 12, 2011

REQUEST YOUR FREE BOOKS!

2 FREE RIVETING INSPIRATIONAL NOVELS
PLUS 2 FREE MYSTERY GIFTS

Love Inspired® SUSPENSE

YES! Please send me 2 FREE Love Inspired® Suspense novels and my 2 FREE mystery gifts (gifts are worth about $10). After receiving them, if I don't wish to receive any more books, I can return the shipping statement marked "cancel". If I don't cancel, I will receive 4 brand-new novels every month and be billed just $4.24 per book in the U.S. or $4.74 per book in Canada. That's a saving of at least 23% off the cover price. It's quite a bargain! Shipping and handling is just 50¢ per book in the U.S. and 75¢ per book in Canada.* I understand that accepting the 2 free books and gifts places me under no obligation to buy anything. I can always return a shipment and cancel at any time. Even if I never buy another book, the two free books and gifts are mine to keep forever.

123/323 IDN FDCT

Name _____ (PLEASE PRINT)

Address _____ Apt. #

City _____ State/Prov. _____ Zip/Postal Code

Signature (if under 18, a parent or guardian must sign)

Mail to the **Reader Service:**
IN U.S.A.: P.O. Box 1867, Buffalo, NY 14240-1867
IN CANADA: P.O. Box 609, Fort Erie, Ontario L2A 5X3

Not valid for current subscribers to Love Inspired Suspense books.

**Are you a subscriber to Love Inspired Suspense
and want to receive the larger-print edition?
Call 1-800-873-8635 or visit www.ReaderService.com.**

* Terms and prices subject to change without notice. Prices do not include applicable taxes. Sales tax applicable in N.Y. Canadian residents will be charged applicable taxes. Offer not valid in Quebec. This offer is limited to one order per household. All orders subject to credit approval. Credit or debit balances in a customer's account(s) may be offset by any other outstanding balance owed by or to the customer. Please allow 4 to 6 weeks for delivery. Offer available while quantities last.

Your Privacy—The Reader Service is committed to protecting your privacy. Our Privacy Policy is available online at www.ReaderService.com or upon request from the Reader Service.

We make a portion of our mailing list available to reputable third parties that offer products we believe may interest you. If you prefer that we not exchange your name with third parties, or if you wish to clarify or modify your communication preferences, please visit us at www.ReaderService.com/consumerchoice or write to us at Reader Service Preference Service, P.O. Box 9062, Buffalo, NY 14269. Include your complete name and address.

LISUS11

*When David Foster comes across an unconscious woman
on his friends' doorstep, she evokes his natural born
instinct to take care of her.*

*Read on for a sneak peek of A BABY BY EASTER
by Lois Richer, available April, only from Love Inspired.*

"You could marry Davy, Susannah. He would look after you. He looks after me." Darla's bright voice dropped. "He had a girlfriend. They were going to get married, but she didn't want me. She wanted Davy to send me away."

David almost groaned. How had his sister found out? He'd been so careful—

"I'm sure your brother is very nice, Darla. And I'm glad he's taking care of you. But I don't want to marry him. I don't want to marry anyone," Susannah said. "I only came to Connie's to see if I could stay here for a while."

"But Davy needs someone to love him. Somebody else but me." Darla's face crumpled, the way it always did before she lost her temper. David was about to step forward when Susannah reached out and hugged his sister.

"Thank you for offering, Darla. You're very generous. I think your brother is lucky to have you love him." Susannah brushed the bangs from Darla's sad face. "If I end up staying with Connie, I promise I'll see you lots. We could go to that playground you talked about."

Susannah's foster sister Connie breezed into the room. "I'm so glad to see you, Suze. But you're ill." She leaned back to study the circles of red now dotting Susannah's cheeks. "You're very pale. I think you need to see a doctor."

"I'm pregnant." The words burst out of Susannah in a rush. Then she lifted her head and looked David straight in the eye, as if awaiting his condemnation.

SHLIEXP0411R

But it wasn't condemnation David felt. It was hurt. He'd prayed so long, so hard, for a family, a wife, a child. And he'd lost all chance of that—not once, but twice.

How could God deny him the longing of his heart, yet give this ill woman a child she was in no way prepared to care for?

Although David has given up on his dream of having a family, will he offer to help Susannah in her time of need? Find out in A BABY BY EASTER, available April, only from Love Inspired.

SHLIEXP0411R